CRaZY as a Run oveR Dog . . . But Don't BLame it aLL on the Animals

Mike Rowland

Lulu Publishing Services rev. date: 4/24/2014

Contents

HOLIDAYS

Dedication

For my mother.
I wish you could be here to see this.

Foreword

I WAS SITTING AT AN OUTDOOR gathering shortly after moving to a new town where my family and I were beginning the process of making new friends. Being the local high school principal helped, but I suspect building new relationships isn't any easier for adults than it is for children. The month was November. The year escapes me.

Seated at my table was the publisher of a local newspaper. It just so happened that his wife was a teacher at my school, and being the opportunist that I am, I leveraged that relationship to let him know that I might be interested in writing an opinion piece for the paper on a regular basis if the opportunity ever arose.

As fate would have it, his newspaper had an opening for a community columnist. He recommended I send a sample or two of my work so he could share it with his editor. The rest, as they say, is history.

Some people write books to tell stories, both fiction and fact. Others out of some deep desire to be published. This book is a compilation of some of my favorite columns over the years. Mostly, the words I have written share stories about my own life and how it connects to the world in some meaningful way. My opinions are always my own and never meant to hurt feelings or be demeaning to other people. Too many times, opinionists like myself believe the First Amendment gives us the right to say anything without regard for how it impacts others. I couldn't disagree more.

So if I have offended you in any way, please accept my sincerest apology. It has never been my intention to convince you to think like I do but rather to encourage you to think. Period.

I hope you enjoy reading some of what has otherwise become a weekly therapy session for me. In the following pages, it is my desire that you will find comfort, tears, laughter, and shared experiences.

Mostly, I hope you find something to think about.

MY CHILDREN

A Letter to Brian

TODAY MY YOUNGEST SON WILL GRADUATE from high school. As with his brother before him, I am extremely proud of this accomplishment. In Georgia, one third of all students still do not finish high school. Consequently, doing so is a greater accomplishment than one might at first imagine.

I have had the neat experience of watching first hand both of my boys grow up through high school. I handed the first one his diploma, and later this morning I will do the same for the little one, who by the way, is not so little anymore.

The entire experience is at the same time sad and exciting. I thought about trying to describe it exactly, but I figure that only a parent with a similar experience would really understand. You will just have to trust me on that one.

More to the point: The Saturday morning after each of my sons completed his junior year, I began a year-long journey with them of writing one letter per week.

As you might imagine, most weeks I was faithful, but as fate would have it, some weeks found obstacles in the way of my lofty goal. In any event, of the 52 ensuing weeks, I probably wrote them more than 30 letters.

As with my first son, the culmination of this labor of love will involve me copying the letters to a CD and slipping that into one of his bags as he leaves for college. Included in that package will be a letter wishing him well and explaining the significance of the CD.

It is my hope that he will find the time while away from home to read through the letters at his leisure. It took me a year to write them, and most are filled with fatherly advice. I expect it to take some time for him to read them all, but hopefully reading one will coincide with some significant

3

question in his life, and having me around in this way will help guide him to some of the answers of life.

What follows is from that last letter, which coincides with the milestone of high school graduation.

Dear Son,

One year ago I began the journey of writing you weekly during your senior year of high school, and I must tell you that the experience has been more powerful for me than I could have imagined. I expected to share with you great pearls of wisdom, and while I have done that, I am the one who has received the blessing of clarifying my thoughts and dreams for both of us.

Today as you reach another milestone in your life, I share these final thoughts about this day and those to come in your future. I hope you will keep this letter close. While it may not be the most profound advice for living, it does represent the best thinking I can muster given my own life experiences.

From this minute on, always look forward. Reflecting on the past can sometimes lead to keen insight regarding the future, but dwelling on it is a sure recipe for depression and self-pity. I am reminded of what happened to Lott as he took his family from the city with express directions not to look back. His wife did and she instantly turned to a pillar of salt. I may be misrepresenting the symbolism of this event, but it helps to remind me of the foolishness of looking back.

Never hurt anyone on purpose. Like it or not, intend to or not, you will hurt people. Unfortunately, it comes with the human experience. Understand that getting hurt is also part of the human experience, and that will happen to you as well. I wish I could insulate you from the hurt, but I cannot. I do believe that the salve that eases the wounds of human disappointment rests solely in where you place your trust. Do not place your faith in people. They will always disappoint you. Place your faith in God, and you will learn to love people even with all of their faults.

In the final analysis, I have tried to think of one parting nugget to give you that will be the key to unlocking the door of success in your life. I keep coming back to this one simple truth. Be happy.

Now, I am not talking about the kind of happiness that comes from momentary, earthly gain. A new job will make you happy for the moment. A new house will make you happy for the moment. So will a pretty girlfriend, a new boat, immoral living, and loud music.

I am talking about the deep-seeded happiness that comes from spiritual discipline, commitment to others, and service above self. Your generation represents the best of times and the worst of times. You have so many opportunities available to you that never existed for me. That is exciting.

On the other hand, there are so many things out there competing for your time and talent that it scares me to death to think of how you will filter through it all. Not all of the things in which you are invited to partake are good. Evil is still very much alive in our world, and it can find you when you least expect it.

May God grant you the power of discernment so that you might know the difference between those things that will bring you lasting peace and contentment and those that will destroy you with momentary happiness.

Finally, your mother and I love you very much, and that will never change. We will always hold you responsible for your thoughts, words, and deeds, but you will likewise always have a home to come to when you need comfort and safety. That will never change either.

Good luck in your quest to find what works for you, and just in case I have forgotten to tell you lately, you are a fine young man. Don't let anyone ever tell you differently.

All my love,
Dad

A Letter to Steven

I HAVE TWO SONS, AND FOR all practical purposes, they are grown men. They are very different in the way they are hard wired. They have chosen different paths into their future, but I am equally proud of them both.

Obviously, I do not know much about rearing daughters. Arguably, however, I have to believe that growing sons into contributing members of a complex society is different than doing so for girls.

Not, better, worse, or more complicated, mind you; just different.

The Good Lord has granted me great opportunities in life, and one of those was to hand each of my sons his high school diploma. I won't even try to explain what that feels like. I really cannot think of words that would do the event justice.

I am not sure what possessed me to do this, but I wrote each of my sons one letter each week during their final year in high school. I saved the letters and gave them to each child all at one time.

The truth is I don't know if they ever read any of them or not. We have never really talked about it.

But, regardless of any impact it may have had on each of them, that little project was one of the more powerful experiences in my life. If you have children, I encourage you to write them letters. It may mean little to them at the time, but it will change you forever.

This morning, my older son will graduate with a degree in chemistry from GC&SU. Can you believe that? Chemistry. He is the brains in this outfit. I had to Google chemistry so that I could spell it.

Classified Ad: Recent college graduate looking for gainful employment in the field of chemistry. Looking to earn own way. Dad needs a break.

Sorry, I just couldn't help slipping that in.

It goes without saying that I am proud of his accomplishment, so I thought I would take one more stab at a letter to my son:

Dear Son,

I wish I knew the words to say adequately how proud we are of you today. I am a little miffed at the college, however, because they obviously do not understand the Rowland tradition of father handing sons their diploma. I would have thought they would at least have asked if I was interested.

The truth is, however, the entire act of you receiving a credential from someone outside the family is symbolic of one of the great lessons of life. The apron strings that link us to our children become shorter and more tenuous as you grow into adulthood. While I will always be near with a watchful eye, you must now begin the journey of finding your own way.

I did take the liberty of using the newspaper to get out a classified ad so that you might find gainful employment. Hey, if you can't use your influence to help out the family, then what good is having it? Right?

All kidding aside, what follows is as much fatherly advice as I can fit into a few lines. If you ever need more, you always know where to find me.

First, a man's character is the only thing that differentiates him between obscurity and greatness. Starting anew is kind of like getting that first driver's license. The first day your driving record is perfect. The only thing you can do from that point forward is mess it up. By the way, you will mess up. We all do. Your character is the salve that heals the inevitable wounds of life. Covet and protect it. It may very well be the most powerful tool you will use in your relationship with others.

Secondly, accept the fact that life's rewards are not always immediate. Don't ask me to explain it. Just save yourself a lot of disappointment by accepting the fact that much of what you will accomplish in life is more a factor of your ability to persevere than it is any singular event. Tiger Woods may win the Masters, but few people who watch him put on the coveted green jacket see the countless hours of practice and preparation they combine with opportunity to make greatness.

One other thing: I hope you make a lot of money. If you do, give most of it away. Money in and of itself does not accomplish much. What you do with it is your legacy. If you never make much money, that's okay, too. In either case, give some of it to others who do not have the advantages you have been afforded. One of the things that is wrong with this world is that we too often allow our focus to be about "what's in it for me". What's in it for you will depend on how you invest your time, talents, and gifts in others. Invest wisely, but above all, invest.

Finally, twenty-six years ago I remember walking up to my father, putting my arm around his shoulder and asking the question, "How does it feel to see your only son graduate from college?" After all this time, I cannot at all remember what he said.

But, I know how he felt.

One last thing: I went to school to become a teacher. As far as I know, there has been no one else in our family to hold that distinction. You are a chemist. I don't think we have any of those either. Congratulations on your decision to go places where none of us have been. There is a picture that hangs on the wall in my office that speaks perfectly to my hope for your future. It reads "Don't be afraid to go out on a limb. That is where the fruit is".

God bless you in your endeavors as you set out to make your mark on the world.

All my love,
Dad

A Letter to Meghan

THESE ARE EXCITING TIMES AROUND THE Rowland household. I haven't told you this, but my oldest son has accepted a graduate assistantship at Florida State University. Apparently, he has gotten himself accepted into the doctoral program in analytical chemistry, and get this…they are going to pay him to do it.

Go figure.

Anyway, we are all proud of him for his accomplishment, but I have to tell you that I am not at all sure how I feel about him actually leaving home to make his way in the world. And, if you think I have issues, you should talk to his mother.

We have until August to sort through all of that, and I am sure I will have more to say about his adventures in the future.

For now, however, the most exciting part of his life, to me, is the fact that he has found his soul mate. That's right. The young lady he has been dating for the past few years is going to FSU with him, and it looks like there are wedding bells in their future.

I am not sure exactly when, but I do know that my senior name sake dove head first into the conversation that every aspiring husband has to have with the bride-to-be's father. Steven asked Meghan's father if he could marry her, and apparently, he said "yes".

By the way, her name is Meghan.

We love Meghan for a lot of reasons not the least of which is that she is a free thinker, and she gives my know-it-all son a run for his money in the philosophy of life department. She is especially cute when she thinks she can compete with me in the aforementioned philosophy of life category, but I just chalk it up to youthful exuberance and let her think what she wants.

Just kidding, Meghan.

At any rate, Meghan graduates from college today with a degree in psychology. She is very smart which might explain why she thinks she can keep up with me in that philosophy of life thing. Here is a lesson for you all. No amount of schooling can compete with a PhD from the school of hard knocks.

Kids are so cute.

So, now that it looks like Meghan will eventually wear the Rowland name with pride, I thought she might as well be the subject of one of my newspaper columns – a sort of "right of passage" if you will. And, yes, she always reads my columns before they are published, and I did get her blessings before I e-mailed this to my newspaper buddies.

No matter if it is high school or college, graduation is a big deal. The graduation rituals are also important because they represent the way teachers and professors celebrate the latest inductees into the honor society of the educated.

So, later this morning, everyone in my clan will join Meghan's family to celebrate her passage out of one life and into another.

When my own children graduated from both high school and college, I wrote them a letter. Meghan has been around for so long I consider her one of mine, and since my son had the whole "can I marry your daughter" conversation with her father, I figure I might as well pass the custom on to her.

So, here is my letter to Meghan.

Dear Meghan,

Ms. Trudy and I are so proud of you on this special day. While you have been in our lives only a short time, we have long since adopted you into our family. In fact, we think so much of you that we are willing to hand over our first born son. See what you can do with him. I am about out of ideas.

All kidding aside, there are some things I think you should know as you close one chapter in your life and open another. Of course, my advice is worth what you paid for it, so keep that in mind when you decide what of it you will actually use.

First, be happy. I know that sounds like such a trite statement, but as simple as it is, a lot of people mess it up. Just be happy.

Oh, by-the-way, no one can make you happy. The only person who can be responsible for your happiness is you. Your spouse can't do it, your kids can't do it, your job can't do it, the things you own won't lead to it nor will all of your accomplishments. Happiness is your choice.

Secondly, never settle. Simple enough, right? You'd be surprised.

As I approach half a century of life, I am becoming aware that life really is too short. Set your sights on your dreams and chase them. You won't catch them all, but the chase is really half the fun.

Third, get a good dog. I know. It sounds kind of funny, but remember this: as much as I wish it were not true, people will let you down. Even those who love you most. We can't help ourselves. It is just the way we are.

A dog, on the other hand, will never break your heart. He will give his love unconditionally, and expect so little in return. A little food, a little water, a quick pat on the head, and he will wag his tail silly for you. Those of us who love you just can't compete with that.

Finally, you look after that son of mine, and remember that a relationship is less about what you go through and more about how you come out on the other side. I wish I could promise you that the road to Oz is paved in yellow brick. Unfortunately, the road of life has more pot holes in it than I'd care to admit.

That's about as simple as I can make it. Just know that we all have great confidence in your ability to conquer the world.

Oh, and one more thing... Go NOLES!

For Those Things Money Can't Buy

YOU KNOW, ALL OF THE REALLY good ideas are taken. Take my little episode of creative genius below, for example. If I could have been the first to think of the Mastercard "priceless" angle, then my 401k would be recession proof.

Instead, I come along who knows how many years behind the credit card giant, and I am just another creative has-been piggybacking off someone else's good idea. It's depressing.

In fact, I was so put out over the entire "I can't come up with an original idea" thing that I just wanted to send in my closing remarks as my entire article. Short and sweet. Leave the rest blank. After all, I am worth what they pay me.

But I was reminded that my literary idol, Lewis Grizzard, used this very technique one year when Georgia Tech beat our beloved Bulldogs. He gave the score of the game, said he didn't want to talk about it, and then left about seven column inches of blank space to drive home his point. I still think it was the most ingenious commentary on social values I have seen.

My editor, bless her heart, politely pointed out that, while my approach was admirable, it had already been done. Drats. She's right. I hate it when she's right.

So, licking my wounds, I give you my most heart-felt rendition of "priceless". Take that!, Mastercard. I hope you find something in your life that is priceless, too.

Bright sunshine, a clear blue sky, and eighty-three degrees: courtesy of Mother Nature.

Hamburgers, hotdogs, and all the trimmings for 11 of your closest friends and family: $75

A white gold band with nine princess diamonds delivered by the lake while looking up from one knee: $900

To her complete surprise, watching your oldest son ask the love of his life to marry him: Priceless

Fatherhood Isn't all it's Cracked up to Be

BY THE TIME MOST OF YOU read this, we will have packed up the U-Haul, loaded up all of the memories, and pointed our vehicles in the direction of Tallahassee, Florida. My older son and his fiance' are moving to Florida State to begin graduate school, and they are taking a ton of good memories with them.

I recently finished reading <u>Tales from the Dad Side</u> by Steve Doocy. Doocy is a morning anchor on Fox and Friends, and I highly recommend the book for any dad who just wants to confirm that he is not alone on the cradle to adulthood rollercoaster.

The truth is that any of us who have children could have written it. It doesn't take long for those little people in our lives to create some pretty memorable tales.

No, I am not going to write him a letter for everyone in Middle Georgia to read. I have actually already written a letter which I have given to him privately with the directions that it is not to be read until after Tuesday of next week. That is the day his mother and I will load up in Tallahassee and head north with our collective emotional tails tucked between our legs like a dog who knows that eating underwear off the clothes line makes him a very bad dog.

I also gave Meghan her very own letter to keep private as well. Letters are my thing, I guess, and I hope someday they will appreciate them. What I wish for most is that they will pass on the letter-writing tradition when they have children of their own.

I do, however, want to take the time to reflect on what it means to be a dad and on how watching my first born son become a man has affected me.

Let me begin by saying that both moms and dads have a responsibility to rear boys differently than girls. I don't have girls, so I figure I can say that. My point is simply this: Steven's mother and I have taken very seriously our responsibility to develop our son into the kind of man that accepts as his own the responsibility for working hard, keeping commitments, and for providing moral leadership for those he encounters.

My sons and I have an understanding about our relationship that is important and it works for us. It is simply this: I am not their friend. I am their father. Two very different principles.

Now don't get me wrong. I can be friendly. I enjoy laughing and having fun. But, when it comes to being a father, there is no middle ground. I have a job to do, and both of my sons know that they can count on me to do it.

Occasionally, they thank me for it when they see how other parents have allowed the infection of friendship to cloud their judgment regarding accountability and personal responsibility. Those are pretty proud moments for me.

My favorite father role model, Andy Griffith, once told Opie that no matter what happened he would always be his friend. No matter what, they would always be best buds.

That's not how I played it, and I am not sure which one of us was right. I have told my kids that I will not always be their friend. But they can always count on me to be their father.

It is a funny feeling when you realize that you have just finished an entire can of your favorite soft drink without having to share with little runny nosed runabouts who are notorious for backwashing when they drink. If you don't know what backwashing is, then ask just about any parent who has children. They can tell you.

I could do the "it only seems like yesterday" thing and go through memories from potty training to his first Little League homerun to his first car to his first love to college graduation. But that just seems a little corny and besides, that is what you were expecting.

Instead, I just want you to know that there was once a time when I thought that having my children leave home would satisfy me. After all, I could once again sport my favorite pair of underwear anytime I wanted in any room of the house without regard for who might see me.

Now that it's here, it really doesn't feel so good.

My Thighs Hurt, I Have a new PSA, and my Son is Getting Married

I JUST WANT TO LET YOU know that I successfully completed the Torture Trail 10K road race up in Eatonton last week. Now for those of you who are metrically challenged, ten kilometers equals 6.2 miles.

And there is a reason they call it the Torture Tail. There are several hills along the track that are very challenging, but the last mile or so begins with a slight grade that turns into a significant hill near the end.

Just so everyone knows, the fact that the last hill passes in front of the fire station is just a little intimidating. When the race begins, the runner enjoys the easily accomplished, downhill pace in front of the same fire house. On the return trip, one would swear it wasn't even the same road.

But, I made it. In fact, I finished the race with a new personal best time: One hour-six minutes-thirty-eight seconds. I know...not very impressive if you are the runner type, but I figure since I turned fifty-years-old and am now a cancer survivor...well, it was quite an accomplishment for me.

Speaking of cancer, I went back for my first checkup since the last radiation treatment back in February. The doctor said I looked great, and my PSA was 4.88 – not as good as we had hoped, but the doctor doesn't seem to be worried, so I am not going to either.

We will do this again in another three months, and that routine will continue for the next three years. Regardless of what is going on inside my body, I feel great! I really am luck to be alive.

Which reminds me; later today my oldest son will be walking down the aisle of wedded bliss and entering the state of holy matrimony. That's right. We are having a wedding.

Of course I would be dodging my fatherly responsibility if I didn't have some advice for him as he embarks on this new journey in life. So, without further adieu, here goes.

Dear Son,

We have had a lot of father-son chats over the course of your twenty-four -years, and quite honestly, I am not sure what to add at this point. Your mother and I have done all we can to lay the ground work for you to tackle the future, and I must say that you have been a good student and learned your lessons well.

There are, however, a few things I think we should cover before you take, what will perhaps be, the most meaningful walk of your adult life. Most of this is just stuff I believe, and that doesn't mean that you have to believe it, too. I just wouldn't feel right if I didn't say them.

Thing one: A lot of people believe that the marriage union is a commitment between two people to be completely faithful in all things to the bond that brought them together. I do not believe this at all, and I think it is why so many marriages fail.

I looked up the word "commit" in the dictionary. Actually, that's not true. I looked it up on the Internet. Who uses a dictionary anymore? Which reminds me…life is so much different than when your mother and I began our journey twenty-eight years ago. At your age, I couldn't even envision a personal lap top computer. Text messaging hadn't been invented, and you had to be a millionaire to have a phone in your car.

I know times have changed, but some things remain timeless. Anyway, I researched the definition of the word commit. Commit is a verb which means to make a promise; to pledge devotion to somebody or something.

And, therein lies the problem.

I believe that marriage is not a commitment between

human beings at all. It is a vow to God that you will love, honor, and cherish this individual with whom you have chosen to share your life; that you will forsake all others and cleave only unto her for as long as you both shall live.

The fact that you make this promise to God is significant. People are imperfect, make mistakes, and generally cannot be trusted. God is perfect, does not make mistakes, and can be trusted completely. So, the marriage vows that are said we say to God because people break their promises.

You are a good boy, but you cannot avoid the inevitable. You will promise to get milk on the way home and forget...a small broken promise, but a broken one just the same.

And, when life doesn't unravel over the small broken promises, you will promise that special evening on your tenth anniversary. Life will get in the way; work will sneak up on you; you will get distracted, and by the time you realize the promise has been broken, it will be too late.

My point is this: If you depend only on one another for stability in your relationship, the blessing of marriage will just never be what it could be.

Thing two: Marriage really isn't so much about what you go through; it is more about how you come out on the other side. I know that seems a little trite, and thirty years from now seems like a long way off, but you will be surprised at how quickly it sneaks up on you.

During that time, your lives together will be marked by highs and lows. Some will be peaks; some will be valleys; and some will just be blips on the radar screen. A lot of the tough times you went through will be hard to remember. The fun times will be easier.

But the real measure of your relationship will be where you are on that day. What contributions have you made to your community? To your children? To your family? To your work? The world is a big place. What mark did you leave upon it? Together, did you make a difference? Is your circle of influence better because you are in it?

Finally, I don't know how you feel about it, but today is one of those bitter-sweet occasions for me. On the one hand, I have never been prouder of you and your decision to share the responsibility of life with another person. When I think about how hard we worked to rear you guys, seeing you be successful in any endeavor is like hitting a homerun with the bases loaded in the bottom of the ninth inning with two outs to win the seventh game of the World Series.

On the other hand, I realize that today marks a change in my life that is permanent. Oh, it is true that you have been on your own for some time now, making your mark on the world, and beginning to find your own way. But there is something official about the statement, "With this ring, I Thee wed."

The truth is that you will never need your parents like you did before. Father-son outings will become fewer and farther between. It won't be anyone's fault. Life is just funny that way.

But you will always be our son; and now your wife will always be our daughter. And while the miles may separate us and life's experience may change our viewpoints, neither will ever separate us from our love for you and your new family.

Godspeed, my son!

Love, Dad

The Choice to be Happy

WELL, THE WEDDING CAME OFF WITHOUT a hitch; unless, of course, you consider an outside reception held in 110 degree heat a hitch. In case you haven't been keeping up, my oldest boy, Steven, got married last Saturday to Meghan, and the entire event couldn't have been any more perfect.

As the father of the groom, my job is really pretty simple: pay the bill for the rehearsal dinner. That is really about it. The father of the bride has to pay for the wedding, which I have determined from this latest experience, is much more expensive than the rehearsal, and he has to walk her down the aisle.

To me, paying the bill wouldn't be so bad even though it is a big one. But that walking down the aisle thing is just fraught with peril. My luck would be that I would get myself all tangled up in my daughter's dress and quickly become the spectacle of the entire event.

God knew what he was doing when he gave me boys!

Back to the outdoor reception. In spite of the heat, it was just as perfect as the wedding, and I developed an even deeper appreciation for my new in-laws than I had before.

Steve and Fran are responsible for the kind of family into which every dad wishes his son will marry. Steve is a doctor in Athens, and Fran is a horse enthusiast. They live on a little farm out in the country, and they are the most down-to-earth people I know.

The whole "in-law" thing is a little scary for every marriage experience. It is hard enough to deal with the stress of whether each family will like the spouse to be much less the rest of the family. An added plus is Ben and Lauren, my son's new brother and sister-in-law. They are really cool, too.

Ben is Meghan's brother, and Terry and Janet are Lauren's parents. They are pretty cool people, too, and it was a lot of fun getting to know them better over the course of the weekend.

I tell you all of this because I can't think of any greater wish a parent has for his child than to be happy, and what I saw in the faces of my son and his new wife as they held hands, looked deeply into one another's eyes, and pledged their troth was what I consider to be the definition of happiness.

It was really pretty neat, and the entire experience got me to thinking about what it really means to be happy because I know a lot of people who are not.

I went to the trusty internet to look up the definition of happy, and it turns out it is an adjective with many uses but essentially one definition: to experience pleasure, contentment, or joy.

Now, we all talk about all of the things that make us happy. It makes me happy, for instance when the Braves win, football season begins, and my golf swing is working well. I get really happy when my dog pens up after only having to be told once…doesn't happen often, but it makes me happy when it does.

It makes me happy when my wife has my underwear drawer full. I know. It sounds kind of goofy, but you ever have to go hunting for underwear on a Monday morning whilst running behind for work? Ah, the simple pleasures of life.

It makes me happy when my weed eater cranks on the first try, when the grass dries early so I can get my yard work done before lunch, and when the weather is cool…which doesn't happen much once the grass starts growing.

It makes me happy to grill out with friends, take a ride on the boat, and float in the river. It makes me happy when the golf course is green, my tee time is early, and it is cool enough to walk. Golf is really a game that was meant to be played walking. I don't know who screwed up the game with the golf cart, but regardless, I am happy when they have them when it is too hot to walk.

When my children were born, I was happy. So was their Mama. When they moved out, it was a different story, but when they come back home, I am happy again. If they stay more than a couple of days, I am happy when they leave, too.

Come to think about it, there are a lot of things in this world that make me happy. But my good friend Toby Hill taught me that no one is responsible for my happiness but me. No thing or circumstance or individual can make me happy. I am in complete control of whether I choose to be happy or not.

It took me a long time to acknowledge that fact, but the truth of the matter is that I am happy because I choose to be. When I am unhappy, that is my choice, too.

And all of this ran through my head as I watched two really smart, really good looking kids make the choice to be happy; and that made me happy, too.

The Great American Man-Dog Camping Trip

I AM ALWAYS LOOKING FOR AN investment opportunity, and I recently found one to suit me. I bought a little piece of mountain property in Western North Carolina. It was kind of one of those "come see our property and we will give you a twelve-inch TV and a set of steak knives" kind of thing, but I figure for what I paid for it, at least I own a piece of dirt. Given what is going on with the stock market lately, I just prefer to be able to visit my investments.

In case you didn't know, the mountains are my passion. That is hard to believe, I suppose, given the fact that I awake each morning to the beauty of lake living, but there is just something about the mountain atmosphere that I can't shake.

My little piece of mountain heaven has two little streams on it that eventually meet at the rear of the property. As bodies of water go, they are nothing to brag about, but they do make enough noise that you can hear them rolling over the rocky bottom from anywhere on the property.

My goal for the summer is to go visit my little mountain escape at least once each month. So, as fate would have it, Mama had something to do last weekend that didn't include me, and I decided to take Otis and go camping for the weekend.

In case you didn't know, Otis is my chocolate lab, and he weighs eighty-five pounds if he weighs an ounce. And, in spite of his girth, he is still in his puppy year which makes him absolutely a hoot to be around.

Now, I don't take many days off from work, but I figured this to be the Great American man-dog weekend. I, therefore, took off Friday and Monday so that we would have plenty of time to bond and enjoy the mountain majesty.

Our plan was to leave before lunch Friday, take the leisurely four hour trip to our little slice of paradise, and take our time setting up camp. Just so you know, when I mean camp, well, I mean the primitive kind. The only water on the lot is courtesy of Mother Nature, there are no facilities, and the only electricity you will find is the cloud to ground variety that emits from very dark clouds.

In fact, I got so excited about the trip that I started loading the trailer Wednesday. Let's see…my lawn tractor for cutting grass, the weed eater, chainsaw, and shovel…my portable gas grill, two burner Coleman stove, and a gas operated generator. You see a pattern here?

I have more gadgets and motorized pieces of equipment than you can imagine. Just so you know, the generator is for two purposes only: to run my electric pump to pump up the air mattress and to provide power for my electric coffee maker. There are just some home comforts a man shouldn't live without.

Oh, the coolers. Don't forget the coolers; one for food, and one for drinks. There is just something about a camping trip that makes a man's appetite voracious.

Otis always has a voracious appetite, and will most likely eat anything. Lately, his favorite is a stick or one of the pieces of lava rock I recently introduced into my landscape. I am convinced the old boy is part goat because he seems to eat anything that doesn't eat him first. Go figure.

So, I wake up Friday morning, only a few minor things left to load into the truck, hook up the trailer, put Otis in the back of the truck, and hit the road…only one major problem. By mid morning a pretty significant thunderstorm is raining on my parade.

Using the power of the Internet, I watch the weather radar only to determine that this line of thunderstorms is followed by another. Reluctantly, I finally throw in the towel and just resign myself to the fact that my trip will be cut one day short. A minor setback to say the least.

I mentioned my trailer. Hold onto that thought. I will come back to it later.

My determination to make the trip was tempered in great measure by the fact that my oldest son was flying in from California Friday afternoon, and our plan was to have him drive up from Atlanta to spend Saturday night with me. It has really been a long time since we had a father-son outing, and I had been looking forward to that as much as anything.

I won't bore you with the details, but I cannot remember when I had a more rewarding experience. Steven got there around 6:30 PM, and I had two quality, marinated steaks waiting for us to put on the grill. I used my little Coleman stove to heat up some beans, and we both agreed that the steak might have been the best one ever.

Of course Otis thought the steak was pretty yummy, too. I also found out that in addition to rocks and sticks, my little canine friend is somewhat partial to baked beans as well. So after a long afternoon of romping up and down the creek, playing with his big brother, capped off with a meal fit for a king, the little fella was slap worn out.

His human companions weren't in much better shape, and nightfall found us all turning in for the evening. The moon was full and shined brightly through the window of our tent. Otis wanted to sleep inside with us, but I only look stupid. I have seen what the big oaf can do in enclosed spaces, and I had no intention of fighting that all night.

Keep in mind, now, that my little buddy sleeps outside every night. He is an outside dog, so he is entirely used to the entire camping out thing. Apparently, however, he was a little apprehensive about sleeping under unfamiliar stars, and he finally nestled his big behind right up next to me from the outside of the tent.

Big sissy!

Apparently, there were several deer in the area teasing Otis a bit because sometime during father-son chat number eight, we heard a deer blow from what sounded like just across the creek. For two guys who are outdoorsmen at heart, that was pretty cool. Otis survived the night, and we all had a great breakfast on what turned out to be a perfect Sunday morning.

Breaking camp was almost as fun as setting up, and we loaded up my old trusty trailer for the long trip home. I noticed as we hooked up the trailer that those tires looked like they might just be riding on borrowed time.

I tried not to think about it and said a quick prayer that God would get me home without a flat. After all, a spare tire for the trailer would have involved a lot more planning than I am capable of doing.

The trip home was long, but as we turned down my road, I figured I could manage a flat at that point if necessary. Just the same, I asked God one more time to see me the 3.2 miles remaining to my driveway.

You won't believe this, but just as I turned into the drive way I heard a loud bang, and I limped down the driveway with the left tire on my trailer as flat as a pancake.

Now I don't know of anyone who doesn't question the existence of God at some point in their lives. In fact, one of those father son chats we had centered on that exact topic.

I rest my case.

A Letter to Uncle Sam

Dear Uncle Sam:

I have never written you before today because I guess I just figured that you have such big responsibilities that you have better things to do than to read a letter from me. But there are a few things I need you to know, and one favor I need to ask.

I am just a normal American living the American dream. I have a wife of twenty-nine years and two sons, one is a graduate student in college, and the other I will introduce you to later. We live in a modest home, have two cars in the garage, hold down reasonable jobs, and always pay our taxes on time.

Come to think of it we pay a lot of taxes. Taxes don't bother me that much because I figure they are a small price to pay for the privilege of living in a free, democratic society. Not only that, but I have been blessed with much good fortune, and I take seriously my responsibility to help look after others.

I have an extended family that is close, I am in reasonably good health, and I have a dog that loves me. I pay my bills on time, go to church most Sundays, and volunteer in my community when I can. I just can't imagine a life much better than this.

You have taken a lot of criticism lately about everything from national security to health care. I suppose that is to be expected given the fact that the world is more complicated than ever before, and my generation of Baby Boomers can be about as selfish as a group of two year olds in a candy store.

All in all, however, I think you do a pretty good job. I just wanted you to know that.

I also think America is still the greatest nation on earth. We enjoy personal liberties that are second to none. We haven't quite figured out how to look after everyone, but the world still sees us as the Land of Opportunity. That must be true because so many people risk their lives to cross our borders every day.

I know we are in a little slump right now, but this nation has proven many times over that it is tough, strong, and resilient. Our past is full of great ideas, marvelous inventions, and really good times.

We have a few black eyes, too, but we have always seemed to overcome the human tendency for self-destructive behavior to emerge stronger and better than before. I see no reason to believe that we are not capable of that again.

Anyway, I just wanted you to know that I haven't given up on you. I consider myself to be a loyal patriot. I proudly fly the flag of this great nation in my yard, I get chill bumps and a little teary eyed at the playing of our National Anthem, and I have great confidence in the principles of government outlined in our Constitution and in those elected to support and defend it.

Oh, one other thing. In a few days I will deliver to you my youngest son to be sworn in as a sailor in the United States Navy. He is tall, blonde, handsome and twenty-one-years-old. He is a really good kid, represents his parents and family well, and still says "I love you" at the end of every phone call. Moms expect that, I guess, but for a dad, that is pretty cool.

Like most kids his age, he is both complicated and simple; squared away and searching; confident and timid. He has a heart for others and is instantly attracted to every stray animal that wanders up. Funny thing is that those strays seem to have a natural attraction to him, too. I am not sure what that means, but I am absolutely convinced it is special.

I think in a lot of ways, every dad hopes for his son a life that he himself never led. Some dads live out major league baseball careers through the Little League experiences of their sons. I never served in the military, but at nearly fifty-one-years- old I often wish I had. My son has chosen that path for himself, and no matter how hard I try not to, I suspect I will see his accomplishments as in some way fulfilling certain dreams or obligations that I never achieved. Perhaps I am supposed to resist the temptation to think that way, but right now it feels pretty good.

I mentioned previously that I consider this nation to be great. I understand fully that it did not become that way without sacrifice. While my son will receive training and skills that will hold him in good stead for the remainder of his life, I am keenly aware of the fact that he will be standing watch over the very freedoms that I covet.

It scares me to death to think of that responsibility placed squarely upon his shoulders – not because I doubt his readiness for the task, but because I know it is a dangerous job. I guess there are some feelings a father can just never shake.

So, here's the deal. You look after my boy. Make sure he has everything he needs to defend you, and I have every confidence you will not be disappointed. Push him to do better than he thinks he is capable because every young man needs that.

I have been thinking a lot lately about all of the contributions I have made to this country over the years. Most days I think I have done okay. On others, I know I could have done more.

But today I give you the best I have to offer: my flesh and blood. I charge you to take that responsibility as seriously as have his mother and I. And when his commitment to his country is complete, you send him back to me better than you found him, and I will consider us square.

My wife and I pray for our children every day. We will

now add to our pray list the sons and daughters of all who serve in an effort to protect and defend our way of life. We also pray for our nation because in spite of our faults, God has blessed us mightily.

So, here's to you, Uncle Sam. May God bless our people, and may God bless the United States of America.

Sincerely,
A Proud Father of a Sailor

And all This Time I Thought
I was the Teacher

THIS PAST MONDAY MAMA AND I dutifully delivered our youngest son to the Naval Recruiting Office in Macon so that he could be transported to MEPS in Atlanta to begin his journey into the United States Navy. By the way, MEPS stands for Military Entrance Processing Station. I thought the education business was alphabet happy, but I think the United States Military has us beat.

We also took off to Atlanta so that we could take advantage of the opportunity to see him sworn in on Tuesday morning. We spent a couple of hours with him Tuesday as he processed in and prepared to take the oath.

Then it happened. As we stood at the back of the room, a uniformed officer of the U. S. Army repeated the oath to about fifteen or twenty new enlistees, representing all branches of the service, and the act was official. My baby is a sailor. If you've never heard the words of the oath or contemplated its meaning, then I recommend you take the time to read it. Here are the exact words:

I, Brian Rowland, do solemnly swear that I will support and defend the Constitution of the United States against all enemies, foreign and domestic; that I will bear true faith and allegiance to the same; and that I will obey the orders of the President of the United States and the orders of the officers appointed over me, according to regulations and the Uniform Code of Military Justice. So help me God.

Now I have to tell you that I was there when my little fella made his grand entrance into this world. I was there when he took his first steps and when he spoke his first words. I lived through potty training, emergency room trips, and second grade.

Second grade was a particularly troubling year because it was the year we discovered the little rascal was really his father's son. He couldn't sit still in class, homework was a foreign language, and mischief was his middle name.

He was cute, however, which goes a long way toward helping any little boy navigate the perils of second grade. Looking back on it, second grade was a tough year for me, too. Seems to run in the family, but I digress.

I managed to live through a learner's license, the driving test, and turning him loose with his first car. Girls, first dates, and broken hearts followed, and we managed to live through all of that, too.

Heck, I even lived through the fact that he got hit by a car in the third grade. I almost forgot that.

That little episode resulted in a broken leg, surgery, and a couple of stainless steel pins, not to mention the near fatal heart attack I suffered when his mother called to tell me what had happened.

It's kind of funny now, but it was a dark day then. I did almost faint when the doctor removed the cast for the first time, and I saw the pins sticking out of his injured leg. Again, I digress.

I watched his first high school baseball game, celebrated the first time he struck out an opposing batter, and was the first one out of my seat to watch his first homerun sail over the left centerfield fence.

During his senior year of high school, I got up early most Saturday mornings and wrote him a letter which I saved to a computer disc and gave him as he left for college. I doubt seriously that he ever read them all or that anything I wrote in them had a profound effect on his future. I am absolutely sure, however, that they changed me forever.

I had the distinct honor of handing my child his high school diploma, one of the very cool experiences of my life. His mother and I later delivered him to college and helped him move into a dorm for his first true adventure away from home. I also was there to comfort and guide him when he came home three months later a little dejected because the entire experience hadn't worked out well.

I gave him guidance as he took his first full time, benefit paying job as a car salesman. I watched the highs of big paydays, the lows of a bad market, and rejoiced inside when they laid him off and he went back to school. The car business taught him lessons that I could never have bought at any college.

He did go back to school long enough to earn a two-year degree and to realize that the formal education that the rest of his family had achieved just wasn't for him. Honestly, I am not the least bit disappointed that he decided to travel a different path than his parents. Something about his divergent spirit inspires me.

I actually have no idea how long it takes to say the military oath of allegiance. In reality it must have only been a few short seconds, but during that time I had the opportunity to think about all of the aforementioned things and without even realizing what was happening I felt a grin break out across my face and a tear run down my check that must have made everyone in the room wonder what I was up to.

Now I am about five feet, eight inches tall on a good day, but what I was up to in that meeting room seemed about ten feet tall. As proud as I was at that moment, the quick reality of what I had witnessed came to pass as my newly enlisted sailor grabbed his bag, hugged his mother and me, said "I love you", and headed for the bus.

The lump in my throat almost choked me, but here is what that entire experience taught me. All these years I thought it was I who had been teaching my son about honor, loyalty and commitment. In reality, it had been he who was the teacher all along.

God speed, my son.

What the Sailor's Creed Means to Me

I MAY HAVE RECENTLY TOLD YOU that my youngest son has joined the United States Navy. He enlisted under the Delayed Entry Program back in July, and he leaves for basic training in January of next year. He will spend almost three months in Great Lakes, Illinois.

Now I am not exactly sure where Great Lakes, Illinois is, but I am certain it is a long way from here. I do, however, know the general direction in which one would travel to get there from here, and I know it will be colder than a polar bear's nose stuck to an iceberg up there at the beginning of a new year.

Be that as it may, his mother and I are very proud of him and happy that his life has a new found direction. It took Mama a little while to come around, but she now proudly displays a bumper sticker in her rear window that boldly proclaims that she is a proud parent of a sailor.

The Navy is pretty smart. They know it is awhile before he has to report, and just to be sure he doesn't experience cold feet, they have him report once or twice a month so they can keep an eye on him. Knowing young people like I do, trust me, that is pretty smart.

Of course, I ask him after every visit what all they do. Just in case you don't know my little guy...who by the way is a little over six feet tall and weighs just under 200 pounds...is not widely known for his engaging conversations. Text him a question, and that is another matter. But trying to get information out of him is like pulling teeth.

Regardless, I did get him to tell me that one of his assignments in the coming weeks was to write an essay on what the Sailor's Creed means to him. I had no idea that there was such a thing, but I must admit I am not surprised. After all, any organization worth its salt has a creed.

Of course I asked him to repeat the creed for me which he was able to do without hesitation. I looked it up later on the Internet, and as I read the words and heard them in his voice rolling through my mind, it gave me chills. The kind of chills I get at a football game when the band plays the National Anthem.

The Sailor's Creed is exactly five sentences. Simple, straight forward, concise; so I decided to take a stab at it myself. Here is what the Sailor's Creed means to me sentence by sentence.

I am a United States Sailor.

I mentioned earlier how proud my wife and I are of our son. That simple statement of who I am is full of pride. For me, I am a man; I am a teacher; I am a husband; I am a father; I am a community member. All of those statements carry with them a deep sense of responsibility to go along with all of that pride. An understanding of one without the other misses the point.

A United States Sailor is a man or a woman; a son or a daughter; a mother or a father; a face with a name; and a United States Sailor deserves the respect of every individual who sleeps under the freedom he or she provides.

I will support and defend the Constitution of the United State of America, and I will obey the orders of those appointed over me.

It concerns me that in the 200 plus years since our Constitution was written many Americans have lost the significance of its doctrine. The Constitution is arguably the most important document in American culture, and we seldom give it much attention in our daily lives.

It is the definition of who we are as a civilization, and it contemplates that being an American is a corporate event that is bigger than our individual importance. I can think of no responsibility higher than that of supporting and defending America's Founding Document. We should all be so inclined.

The second part of that sentence is perhaps just as powerful. First, it acknowledges that each of us has an authority over us. It could be your boss at work, or your parents, or your God; but make no mistake, we are all second to someone.

And without apology, the Sailor's Creed recognizes the important of obedience. Obedience is an act of humility that is quickly becoming an idea that describes a bygone day. We have somehow convinced ourselves that we don't have to follow the rules; that the rules apply to everyone but us; and that being subservient to an authority figure is in some way an act of weakness.

This one sentence should become the defining sentence of every human being's personal creed.

I represent the fighting spirit of the Navy and all who have gone before me to defend freedom and democracy around the world.

I think it is important to recognize that this big old world we live in is interconnected. We can no longer live in isolation of the forces of evil that mean to harm our democratic way of life. As much as I wish it wasn't so, defending freedom can only be accomplished from a position of strength. Make no mistake about it. We live in the most powerful nation on Earth. We have a responsibility to acknowledge that spirit and respect those who have defended it before us.

I proudly serve my country's Navy combat team with Honor, Courage, and Commitment.

When I think about my own child and his Navy career, I focus on the fact that he will receive some of the best training in the world at his chosen vocation. But this statement reminds me that defending America and my way of life is the primary job of a Sailor. Something about the words "combat team" have the sobering effect of reminding me that it takes a gun to defend freedom, and guns kill people.

Honor, Courage, and Commitment. I can think of no greater ambition than to live a life grounded in these concepts.

I am committed to excellence and fair treatment of all.

I couldn't have said it any better myself.

The Box, an Address, a Sheep's Skin, and Where's my Check?

In case you hadn't noticed, there has been a change in the way we do business around here. I am not really sure when it happened, but the economy in our area changed from one that relies mostly on manufacturing to one that focuses on service. One only has to look at the number of restaurants, hotels, golf courses, and resorts dotted across our community as proof that the service industry is where our future lies.

If you are like me, however, your experiences with those individuals who are charged with upholding this service attitude in its most prominent light are suspect at best. Too many times I call to get help because my power bill doesn't look just right, or a product I purchased from a local merchant didn't live up to my expectations, or the insurance company refused to pay when I know it should have only to be greeted with a snotty-nosed attitude on the other end of my phone call.

I don't have many buttons in this world, but that is one of them.

Three things happened to me recently, however, that have restored my faith in the service industry. Let me explain.

I have been telling you for the last couple of weeks about my youngest son's journey into the Navy. In fact, at the printing of this column, we are just shy of two weeks of what might possibly be the longest gap between conversations or at least a reassuring text message.

Of course Mama and I had been conditioned to expect such a blackout so we were ready. We had been told, however, that our son's civilian belongings would show up at our house in a box and that most probably we would have a note from him at least giving his mailing address so that we could send him cards and letters during the cell phone slash communication with the outside world black out.

Almost a week to the day from his departure, and true to the Navy's word, the infamous box showed up on my porch. I got home from work first that day, and immediately opened "the box".

Let's see…belt, holey jeans, boxers, cell phone, Ipod with ear buds, Georgia Boots….nope. No letter. No card. No mailing address at all.

Now my wife had already given explicit instructions when I left the house that morning that should the sun set without her knowing how to send a letter to her baby boy, then I was to call the recruiter to find out what the devil was going on. Trust me. That is the G-rated version of what she said so I got the message loud and clear.

Having inventoried the contents of the box and finding it lacking, and knowing that my wife was most probably on her way home, I had no intention of letting the sun set without at least making an attempt to follow my orders from twelve hours earlier. I called Petty Officer Ransaw down in Macon, explained to him my predicament…I might have even mentioned something about hell having no fury like a woman's scorn…and within minutes he had me the coveted information we had been awaiting for nearly a week.

I thanked him for saving me from the wrath of a love-sick mama, and took a deep breath. Whew. That was close. And not one cross word, not one silly excuse, not one menacing scowl.

Rewind to a few weeks prior, and my now dutifully stationed little Seaman Recruit finished enough credits at Georgia Military College to receive a diploma. Of course it was touch and go for a while, and getting him to actually fill out the paperwork so that he could graduate was about like pulling eye teeth.

Finally, the Friday before he left the following Tuesday, he went to the college, ran down all of the paper work, paid his fees, and came home quite proud of himself because in the battle of hanging diplomas on the wall, he was not going to get skunked. Truth be told, we were all sort of proud of him. I think he was pretty proud of himself. We promised to bring the diploma with us when we make the trip to see him graduate from basic.

The same day we shipped him out, a letter from GMC arrived at the house that said, "Hold the phone on that graduation thing" – paraphrased slightly, of course. "You didn't complete all of the requirements."

Now, I had my doubts all along. I was aware of the requirement to which the college referred, and I was equally aware of the fact that Little Dude hadn't met it. Of course I was furious, not so much at the college, but more at my son for not meeting the requirement and waiting around until the last minute to take care of things.

I was disappointed for him, too, but Mama made me promise to at least check into it the next day. Why do I always get stuck with the dirty work?

So late the following afternoon, I called Sally. I explained my situation to Sally, told her I realized what had happened wasn't her fault even though I felt the college could have stopped the whole application for graduation thing if someone had been paying attention, and asked her if she could at least refund me the graduation fee since it didn't look like the whole Pomp and Circumstance thing was going to happen after all.

Now Sally could have been argumentative and disagreeable, but she was not. She looked through her information, made a few clicks on her keyboard, and somewhat apologetically admitted that the requirement that allegedly stood between my son and his diploma really wasn't a requirement after all.

Man did I need to hear that! My boy had been telling me all along that the requirement had been dropped, and I just figured he had misunderstood. I know, I know. I should have had more faith, but I have been living with this kid all of his life. After all, he is his father's son, and that sounds just like me when I was his age.

A few days later, Sally left me a nice voicemail saying that the diploma was out for signatures and that she would mail it to me when she got it back. She also asked me to thank my son for volunteering to protect her when I take his diploma later this spring.

Sally, you are my hero.

I'll make this last one short. I rented a storage building from a local merchant, and about a month ago I finally got it cleaned out. I took the lock by to retrieve my deposit and inquired into the fact as to whether I should get some money back since I had paid a month's rent in advance.

The nice lady behind the desk agreed with me, and said I could expect my check in about a month. Well, a month passed and no check, so...you guessed it! I called Kelly.

Kelly remembered my situation and without hesitation promised to look into my pending rebate, and this she did with a friendly tone and a pleasing disposition. I didn't even have to threaten to write nasty things about her in the newspaper!

So, hats off to Petty Officer Ransaw, Sally, and Kelly. Thank you for restoring my confidence in those who treat others well and for your commitment to serve folks like me who need you.

Emotions Only a Parent can Understand

THERE ARE A LOT OF CHARACTERISTICS that make really good authors. For me, I like to read the works of individuals who can capture the essence of an idea or a moment through the use of descriptive words or phrases. Obviously, I am more engaged when I can see in my head what the author attempts to portray on paper.

It is not hard, for example, to describe the colors of fall leaves or the sound of rain falling against the leaves of summer trees. We all have some prior experience or some frame of reference that helps us to use our mind's eye to validate what a writer sees through the written word.

Or perhaps our mind has a recorded image or sound or smell that triggers a memory that relates to the writer's descriptive text thus making the connection between the two almost real. It is in these cases that the essence of what it means to learn through reading is achieved.

It is much more difficult, however, to capture in writing the essence of a feeling or an emotion. Although each of us has experienced joy, or loss, or pain, I believe the mind's eye can often contaminate what the writer means for us to see as our past experiences compete for their own place in our stream of consciousness.

I say all of that to make this point: This is a column about emotion. So I warn you up front that my attempt to help you see or experience certain emotions as I have experienced them may be feeble at best. Bear with me as I give it my best shot.

My first summer job was working for a local recreation department in my hometown. I was fourteen-years-old, and the work consisted of two primary functions. The first involved daytime work cutting grass, lining off ball fields during the summer, and other odds and ends, usually accomplished outside, in the blistering heat.

The second part of my job included evening work - keeping score for baseball and softball games while at the same time being responsible for the overall management of the particular facility being used. In a lot of ways, that began my journey into the people business. When I finally clocked out of that part-time job some eight or ten years later, I had learned more about parents and their children than I had bargained for.

Looking back on nearly forty years of public service that mostly involved parents and children, I wish I had kept count of all of the ballgames I attended. There must have been literally thousands of them.

I have seen just about every interaction you can imagine between coach and umpire, parent and coach, parent and umpire, player and coach, and every combination in between. What I remember most about them all is that by the time I was sixteen-years-old, I had come to the conclusion that a person who doesn't have children of their own just cannot understand what it feels like for a parent to feel as though their child has been wronged.

Some thirty-five years later, I have likewise concluded that the joy of seeing one's children succeed is equally elusive for those individuals who are not parents.

Case in point: My wife and I recently attended our youngest son's graduation from Navy boot camp. I am not really sure what I expected because after nearly nine weeks of not seeing him and having very little personal contact, just seeing his smiling face would have been enough.

What I experienced was perhaps one of the most emotional moments in my life.

Now I love both of my children, and the word pride doesn't begin to touch how I feel about rearing two little boys to be young men. They are both responsible, caring adults who are well on their way to making a mark in the world.

And I had been sitting in the bleachers of the reviewing hall for nearly two hours when the large doors at the rear of the hall raised and the various units assigned to this graduation began to march past the viewing stand. My son was in the next to the last unit, so I hardly noticed the first two or three as they passed by, but when I looked into the second row of Unit 112 and spotted my sailor underneath his "Dixie Cup", I just about lost it.

A lump the size of Texas filled my throat, and tears began to stream down my face and settle in the corner of my mouth. Heck, I get a little teary eyed just remembering the moment.

His head was turned my way, he spotted his mother and me at about the same time, and that sheepish grin he keeps stowed cleverly for display on occasions when he himself knows he has nailed it trumped his intuition to keep a straight face. Although there were hundreds of parents and families represented at that ceremony, it was as if my kid was the only one on stage.

I wish I could somehow make you understand the conflicting emotions of pride for my child and worry for his future. In spite of the pomp and circumstance, in spite of the square jaw and broad shoulders, in spite of the Navy band playing those great marching songs, in spite of the spit and polish, my son's new job is to defend his country.

As I listen to the news on the radio or watch the accounts of violence, lawlessness, anarchy, and rebellion on TV, I am reminded of just how dangerous our world is right now. I am also reminded that U. S. forces are often called upon to protect the liberties that, as Americans, we take for granted.

So I apologize for not being able to adequately communicate my emotion, but if you are a parent, then I am sure you understand.

A Letter to Morgan

IF YOU WERE KEEPING UP WITH my family and their escapades over the holidays, you know that my little boy got engaged. Just for the record, my little boy is somewhere north of six feet tall and probably weighs somewhere in the neighborhood of 190 pounds. In fact, both of my boys outgrew their dad a long time ago, but that is a story for another day.

So the Monday before Christmas, Brian dropped to one knee while the rest of us looked on under the ruse of taking Christmas pictures and asked the love of his life to marry him. Pretty cool. A special thanks to our neighbors, Donna and Terry, for letting us stage the entire scene on a big rock located smack dab in the middle of their yard.

Her name is Morgan. Now we have a daughter-in-law named Meghan and a soon to be daughter-in-law named Morgan, and the most fun I had over the week everyone was home together was listening to Mama call Morgan Meghan and Meghan Morgan. How is that for alliteration?

My brainiac daughter-in-law had the most practical solution to this disturbing dilemma. Just call for M Square, and they will both come running. They are all really fun to be around, and we adore Morgan as if she were one of our own…which I guess technically she will be soon.

If you are a regular reader of my column, you will also know that at significant times in the life of my family, usually involving significant events, I have written each of my children a letter. I once even wrote a letter to my wife. Of course there is no fun in writing a letter if you don't have a newspaper column in which to publish it.

I wrote Meghan a letter when she agreed to marry Steven, and I even wrote letters to them all when they graduated from high school and college. For the most part, my family has been appreciative of the letters I write even if I share them with who knows how many readers in the Middle Georgia area.

I guess that is just one of the occupational hazards of being a Rowland.

So here is my letter to Morgan. Somebody probably forgot to tell her the newspaper gig came with the deal.

Dear Morgan,

When Steven got married, I didn't think so much about losing a son because I had another one to fall back on, but you are getting the last one I have. Just knowing that I entrust the heart of my Little Buddy to you should be enough to communicate to you your acceptance into our family, but just in case it isn't, you should know how proud Miss Trudy and I are of you two and your commitment to a long and prosperous life together.

Notice I didn't say happy. I wish I could tell you that every minute of married life will be peaches and cream, but it probably won't. And if you have chosen a relationship with my son, or anyone else for that matter, because you think he will make you happy, then you will most likely be disappointed.

Happiness is one of those things that too many adults misunderstand. No one can be responsible for your happiness but you. A spouse won't make you happy, children won't make you happy, money won't make you happy...although it can come close...just kidding...a big house and a fancy car won't make you happy. Happiness is something you must find from within and take personal responsibility for securing every time God gives you another sunrise and nightfall to experience.

It sounds kind of corny, but happiness really is a state of mind and heart, and while there are many things in this life you cannot choose to alter, your attitude and the way you view those around you is one of them. Choose to be happy.

I think a lot of people misunderstand the covenant relationship that defines marriage as a religious act as opposed to a secular event. It is easy to believe that when he looks into your eyes at the altar that this son of mine will make promises he will never break. If you think about it, he has probably already promised you things that he did not or could not deliver. That is why I believe the covenant that you enter into in the wedding ceremony is between you and God as opposed to you and the other person. That is why they are called vows and not promises. A vow to God in the presence of witnesses creates a level of accountability that doesn't exist in a promise.

Take your vows seriously but not your promises so much. I guarantee you will both break promises which leads me to my next piece of advice. Learn to forgive. It's not as hard as you think.

Finally, my good friend a Great American Toby Hill taught me that marriage is not so much what you go through but how you come out on the other side. I would try to explain that, but my suspicion is that it takes someone looking back from the other side to understand it. Just know that it is true, and let your life's ambition be to make it to the other side so that you can look back. I hope I am still around so you can tell me how it looks.

Oh, one other thing before I go. I have thought a lot over the years about love and what love means. I love springtime, riding in my boat, and being close to my dog. I love long walks with my mate, trips to the mountains, and watching the sunrise over the lake. I love hotdogs, good friends, and cold beer. Come to think of it, Tom T. Hall wrote a song about all of the things he loves. Growing up, it was one of my favorites.

But somehow being married is about more than love. It is about commitment. Apparently, marriages don't last much anymore, and I think it is because we love too much and we commit too little. Commitment doesn't always suggest that we will agree or that our time together will always be perfect.

But it does contemplate that when bad things happen or disappointment comes our way or when pain and loss invade our happiness that sticking together is better than being apart.

My hope for you and Brian is a life filled with every opportunity to experience love and honor commitment. And just know that as the newest member of the family, you have to feed the dog when we go out of town…by the way, Otis says "Hey".

All my love,

Dad

The "C" WORD

The Family Conference Call
that Changed Everything

MY MOTHER IS DYING OF CANCER. There. I said it. Somehow, I thought it would make me feel better, but it really doesn't.

Four years ago we began the up and down rollercoaster of a life with cancer. I still remember the phone call that delivered the news, a three way call with me and my sister.

At the time, I lived three hours away, and my sister lived two thousand miles away. I knew when my mother got us both on the phone at the same time that what she had to say could not be good.

I really figured she was cutting one of us out of the will. I would have bet it would be me until my sister moved her family two thousand miles away to the great state of Utah. Needless to say, it takes a few days for the full weight of the "C" word to sink in.

My oldest son was graduating from high school that May. The bad news came in March or April. I can't really remember which, and I guess the exact month is of little consequence now.

But, my mother made the decision not to let anything stand in the way of her seeing that graduation ceremony, so the first round of chemotherapy did not begin until June.

As a high school principal, I have had the good fortune to be the person who handed both of my children their high school diploma. For me, that has been a real highlight of my life.

Both of my boys graduated from schools with only one high school in the county. I guess that made us all big fish in a small pond. It also created a center-stage experience for me as principal. I suspect my mother wanted to see that as much as she did her grandchildren graduate.

If there is one thing I now know about watching your children grow up it is the pride that comes from witnessing their success first hand. For my mother, that first graduation gave her the opportunity to see her first born son and first born grandson share that stage. We have never talked about it because we don't have to. I understand it perfectly.

The first round of chemo was typical with all of the associated symptoms. There is something about seeing your mother with no hair that is sobering. The radiation that followed the chemo just about did her in.

That was a painful thing to watch, but the treatment slowed down the cancer. We had about a year and a half before it reappeared. This time the cancer that originated in her lungs had spread to her abdomen.

Surgery removed what the doctors could find, and once again, the cancer seemed to be held at bay. But, if there is one thing I have learned it is that cancer has a mind of its own, and almost two years later, it is growing again.

As a closing note, this is one of those articles I have written over time. It took me several weeks to put it together because I could just never seem to get all of my thoughts together at once.

I tried not to cry while I wrote it, but I couldn't help myself. The thought of tear-stained letters seems a bit corny, I guess, and maybe that is why I could not write this all in one sitting, which is my custom. The emotions were just too draining to spend a single amount of time in one place putting it together.

Knocking on Heaven's Door

ONE OF THE TOUGHEST THINGS ABOUT writing a weekly column is the inspiration. When the mood strikes me and the inspiration is hot, this is the easiest gig I've done.

When my mind is blank, which is more often than I would like to admit, writing three paragraphs is excruciatingly painful much less a page and a half in a Word document.

I also struggle with themes. I just never really know how my thoughts or the angle I give them will be received. So, most of the time, I just let if fly and trust that what I write will turn out the way I intended.

What I am about to share with you is intensely personal. I have struggled with whether to do that mainly because I figure most folks could care less about my personal struggles.

But, mostly what I hope you will take away from this column is that you and I have something in common if you have ever watched someone you care about suffer. I can honestly feel your pain.

If you are a regular reader of my work, then you know that my mother has cancer. Last week, my father called me completely out of sorts because he had to call an ambulance to the house. She was really in a bad way, and I proved that you can drive from Eatonton to Warner Robins in an hour.

To make a long story short, I called my sister, who lives in Utah, and encouraged her to come home. From my short assessment of my mother's condition, I had very little hope that she would pull out of it this time. That was on Thursday.

My sister made it home on Friday, and for a short time, things got a little better. But, by Sunday afternoon, my mother's condition had deteriorated to once again fit my definition of hopeless.

My poor daddy has been living this nightmare for about the last three months, and he had had just about all he could take of the hospital experience. My sister and I sent him home Sunday afternoon to rest while we agreed to team up for the all night vigil of looking after my mother at the hospital.

By late Sunday night, my sister and I were convinced that our mother would not last the night. So somewhere around midnight, we climbed into the bed with her, held her hand, and tearfully said goodbye.

As we talked to her about understanding how tired she was of fighting the demon that has ravaged her body both physically and emotionally, her voice softened to a weakened whisper. We tried to help her rest and watched carefully for what we just knew would be her last breath.

It is hard to explain what you are really thinking when you believe you are about to watch your mother die. I know many have done so, but I have struggled with putting into words, even in my mind, the thoughts of those few hours.

At one point, it saddened me to watch the strong spirit of our family weakened to exhaustion by a cell that you cannot even see. On the other hand, I was glad that my daddy was at home. With all he had shouldered, I just could not bear to see that be his last memory of the love of his life. It wasn't really my call, but I just knew it would be easier if he did not have to watch it happen.

When I left the hospital at eleven thirty Monday morning, the same woman that was knocking on Heaven's door a few hours earlier was sitting up in a chair and wanted chocolate ice cream to eat.

Amazing. An absolute miracle. If I hadn't seen it with my own eyes, then I would have never believed it.

When I left her that day, I bent down near her face, placed my hand on her bald head, and said, "You are one tough old woman."

To which she replied, "I try".

"I know you do, Mama. I know you do."

My wife and I just left the house in which I grew up. My sister cooked chicken and dumplings, a family favorite. They might have been her best effort yet.

My mother did not feel very well, but she is slowly regaining her strength. My daddy seemed to be in better spirits, too.

For about forty-five minutes, my sister and I entertained the entire family with the crazy things a woman who thinks she is dying will say and the hallucinations that result from who knows what.

A pretty happy ending, I think, given the circumstances.

Rainbows, Cracker Barrel, and Goodbye Mama

First, let me apologize for missing my column last week. My schedule is somewhat routine, and I try to write my column on Wednesday or Thursday night. I guess, technically, my deadline is probably noon on Fridays. The good folks down at the paper never have really given me an exact date or time. Somehow they must have found out about my proclivity to put off to the last minute any assignment that isn't pressing. After all, why do today what you can put off until tomorrow? Right?

Thursday was a week ago...a date description typically only found in the South...my sister called to tell me that Daddy had called her upset and that she was on her way to the house to see what was going on. I called my dad before she could get there, and he confirmed that our mother, his soul mate for fifty years, had lost her long, courageous battle with cancer.

I cried. I didn't think I would, but I did. In fact, I cried really hard.

Now, don't get the wrong idea. I cry easily. Don't ask me why. Maybe I am a sissy. I like to think that I am overly sensitive to the beauty and wonder that surrounds me, and because of this, I have a unique way of connecting with the universe.

Okay. Maybe I'm just a sissy, but I cry when people get hurt, at sad movies, and when I think about Knowshon Moreno playing in the NFL. I digress...

I last saw my mother the Wednesday evening before she died on Thursday. She was struggling, to say the least, and I remember asking God during my ninety minute ride home to relieve her of her suffering by taking her home.

And she did suffer. A lot. So, I knew that death would be a relief for both her and my father. They both suffered. Still, I cried.

In case you did not know my mother, suffice it to say she was a strong woman. Not in a bad way, but next to me, she was perhaps the most opinionated person I know. My sister eulogized her perfectly by describing anecdotes from our lives that drove home the point.

I don't know who coined the phrase, "Mama is always right", but my family could have easily held the patent. Just think of all the royalties from those Cracker Barrel restaurants around the world. When I think of missing financial easy street, I also cry. My mama would like being remembered that way.

Speaking of Cracker Barrel, that was one of her favorite restaurants, and I will probably never again look at one in the same way. When I left my home town a few days ago, I called my sister to say I was leaving. She and her family had picked up my dad and they were at Cracker Barrel. A fitting tribute, I thought, to the influence my mother had on her family.

I came home after a couple of days of helping my dad around the house. He was about ready for me to go, and most of what had to be done my sister would have to tend to…like cleaning out all of Mama's clothes. That just seemed to me like something a daughter ought to do.

So, I came home to catch up on a few chores that I had neglected because I had spent the last five or six days looking after other folks. The first thing on my list was to cut the grass. I love cutting the grass.

I think I like it most because nobody calls; nobody bothers me. In fact, a number of years ago, one of my boys dated a girl who was at our house and wanted an answer to a question that only I could provide. I was out cutting the grass, and she said something about interrupting me to procure the answer she needed. My son politely explained that nobody interrupts Dad on the lawnmower. Smart move.

I do a lot of thinking while I cut grass, and I thought a lot this week about death, and dying, and my family, and what it all means.

I loved my mother, and I will miss her. A bunch. She could be as cantankerous as on old Model A on a freezing winter morning, but I loved her. In fact we all did. I will miss her, but I am glad the suffering is over.

You know, God gives us earthly bodies as a vessel to do His work. The only purpose we have on this planet is to make it a better place. The way we serve others, the influence we have on our families, the stories they will most assuredly tell about us when the preacher asks for fond memories before preaching our funerals… all of those things are only temporary, and the frail, human body we are given is the means by which we accomplish those things.

If we don't use it for that purpose, then we have wasted perhaps the most wonderful, the most marvelous, and the most magnificent invention God made. My mother's mortality made me think about whether I am using my all too temporary existence on this planet in a way that matters.

My mother spent most of her life getting her way. Up until the day she died, her constitution for having what she wanted was second to none.

Case in point: Shortly after being sent home from the hospital under Hospice care, her condition deteriorated to the point that the Hospice folks decided she didn't have much time left. So, they sent her to a residential center where it was theorized that she would spend the last two weeks of her life.

My mother wanted to die at home…not in a hospital room. So, she willed herself to get better, and two weeks later she sat up in a chair to prove to the doctor that she was well enough to go home. She got her way, and we took her back to the home she had shared with my father for the better part of forty years. She was really good at getting her way.

We all wonder if our loved ones will get to Heaven. I thought about that, too.

After things settled down the Thursday she died, the funeral home folks had left the house, and we all realized we hadn't had anything to eat. We stood on the driveway of my childhood home trying to decide where to go for supper. Almost without warning, a very dark cloud billowed directly over our house and the deep, rolling sounds of thunder emerged from it.

I looked over at everyone else and said, "Well, she got there, and I figure she and St. Peter are arguing over whether she gets in or not."

We all laughed because, in a loving way, each of us had a mental image of the woman who argued about everything being right in her element.

As we traveled to town for supper, just a short distance from the house and spanning the sky to the east was the most perfectly formed double rainbow I have ever seen, and without even giving it much thought, I said to everyone in the car, "Well, it looks like Mama got her way – one last time."

The Nicest Thing Anyone has Said to Me

FIRST OF ALL, LET ME SAY that I have never had a more humbling experience than the nice thoughts and well wishes many of you have expressed since I shared with you my diagnosis of prostate cancer. There is so much bad in the world, and yet my faith in humanity is restored.

In spite of the evil that lurks around the proverbial corner, you should be encouraged, too. There is nothing more gratifying than the power of people caring for people.

It has been three years since I first started sharing my life, my family, and my profession with you in this space. You have been patient and understanding as I have summarily introduced you to each member of my family. My family members have been pretty good sports, too.

I try not to embarrass anybody, but hey…this is journalism. Well, sort of. Did I ever mention I was the sports editor of my high school newspaper?

My teacher was Brenda Littlefield, and we occasionally run into each other on Facebook. She would probably prefer that you not know that, but I refer you to the aforementioned comment on journalism which is code for "there are no rules".

I digress.

You have allowed me to share with you the seemingly mundane episodes of my existence, and as far as I can tell, there is no petition circulating through the Union Recorder readership area to have me censured. That makes me wonder about you guys a bit, but my hope is now and has always been that by sharing the stuff that happens to me, we can all find some common ground on the continent of humanity.

Perhaps by sharing, we have somehow found something in common even though in most cases we have never met personally. After all, isn't that what neighborhood is all about?

So here is the rest of my cancer story.

About two months ago I went for my annual physical. Actually, I went for my first ever annual physical. I am only forty-nine years old, and I am pretty sure that an annual physical exam is for folks a lot older than me. But, I went.

About two days after my physical, Linda, down at the doctor's office called to tell me that my PSA was elevated. She recommended that I see a specialist for further testing which I did post haste.

After a physical exam, the doctor informed me that he detected a small, hard nodule on the right base of my prostate. That, coupled with my PSA value of 5.59 meant that there was a fifty-percent chance that I had cancer.

The only way to find out was a biopsy. Oh joy! I had no idea how that worked, but I was pretty sure it was no cake walk. So, one week later, I learned how it worked.

Ten samples were taken from the right side of my prostate, and ten samples were taken from the left. Every sample on the right was cancer. All of those on the left were clean. I think that was good news, but it's hard to tell. Cancer is cancer, after all.

So how bad is it, you ask? The severity of prostate cancer is determined by what is called the Gleason Score. The score ranges from six to ten with ten being the worst. I am a seven. The doctor said he wished I was a six, but he was glad I wasn't an eight. By the time the score reaches ten, prostate cancer is just a bad disease.

My good Gleason score coupled with my relatively mild PSA number is good news, and the outlook for a full cure is promising. There are several options for treatment, but we really haven't made any decisions. A few more tests are needed to complete the picture.

So this past week, I underwent my first CT scan. My mother, God rest her soul, hated them. She had to have a bunch of them during her unsuccessful bid to conquer lung cancer. In several cases, the folks at the hospital had to sedate her heavily just to get her to agree to the procedure.

My mother spent a lot of days in and out of the hospital. A number of those visits involved CT scans, and I can just see the hospital staff in some back room doing paper, rock, scissors to see who got the dubious honor of being her escort.

Don't get me wrong, I'd take the CT scan over the prostate biopsy every day of the week, but knowing my mother's personality the way I do and now having experienced one for myself, I can see why she hated them.

So early in the morning on the day of my little test, I started drinking nine-hundred milliliters of barium sulfate suspension. Now for those of you who didn't do so well in high school chemistry, let me remind you that barium is a soft metal. Something about drinking a metal that will eventually course its way through the body's plumbing is just a little unsettling.

I tried pouring it into a beer glass, but it didn't work. It still tasted like blueberry chalk. I will tell you this. When I was in the seventh grade, I could convert milliliters to ounces in the blink of an eye. No more, but I can assure you that nine-hundred, as a value of anything, is a lot.

Now I really have no idea exactly how a CT scan works. That is probably as it should be. I do know this. When I got to the place where this test was to take place, they made me drink more stuff that really isn't healthy to ingest, and then they put radioactive dye into my veins.

That was an experience.

The little lady manning the machine said it would make me feel warm. She was right. Sort of. It actually made me feel like I was on fire, and I could feel the fire spread as it coursed through my veins. All the while, I am lying on my back in something that makes Star Trek look more like reality than fiction.

It was during this time that I remembered the fact that this was a test, and for some reason I wished I had studied harder.

The entire experience only took about thirty minutes and really wasn't all that bad. I did notice earlier that I am starting to glow in the dark, and I have a strong attraction to the stereo speakers. Who can figure?

Back to my mother...she was extremely claustrophobic and quick to panic even under the best of circumstances. And laying in that space-aged contraption, I suddenly got a clear mental image of what it must have been like trying to guide her through one of those events. Really good health care professionals are angels in disguise.

So, early next week I will learn the results of the CT scan. I'm not sure, but I think the reason for this scan is to be sure the cancer isn't more pervasive than the early tests indicate. We will keep our fingers crossed on that one.

In a few weeks, I will undergo an MRI to determine the extent of the prostate cancer. We have discussed options for treatment, but the doctor told me we would make decisions later. I am all for that. Why decide today what we can put off until tomorrow?

I will keep you posted, but in the meantime, I really appreciate all of the thoughts and prayers. You all are the greatest, and I know that prayer works. My favorite e-mail so far came from a good friend who told me that she didn't pray all that much, but she figured I was worth praying for. That might be the nicest thing anyone has ever said to me.

Today May be the Only Day

THE CALL FINALLY CAME. ACTUALLY, THAT'S not true. I made the call, but the results were the same. The young radiation technician on the other end of the line communicated enough enthusiasm to fuel a rocket ship from Earth to the Moon and back.

The Karma between us must also be pretty good, because she told me she was picking up the phone to call when I caught her. In my situation, Karma is good.

Oh, just in case you have not been keeping up, I was diagnosed with prostate cancer back in November. If you have been keeping up, then I appreciate the fact that you are a regular reader, and I'm sorry for bringing it up again. You will never know how much I am humbled by the fact that people will actually read, with interest, anything I write.

Back to the call. The sweet young lady on the other end was happy to let me know that my radiation treatments could begin when I was ready.

So, by the time you read this column, I will have had my third treatment. Only 24 to go! Of course everyone I talk to who has been through this tells me that the worst part is over. The treatments are the easy part. I suppose we will see.

Now, for a lot of people, this whole getting cancer thing is a very private venture. Perhaps that is as it should be, but I have decided to make my condition and treatment as public as possible. My hope is that by drawing attention to prostate cancer and the simplicity of early detection, maybe a few lives will be saved.

I talk about it to my friends. I write about it in the newspaper. I post my experience on Facebook. Heck, I will even talk to any group or organization you represent if you will only ask me. Just contact my booking agent….wait a minute….I don't have a booking agent. Okay. Just contact the newspaper. They know how to get a hold of me.

Footnote: "a hold of" is not a grammatical mistake. It is the southern vernacular for "contact". Make the substitution for yourself. See. It works.

My good friend Toby Hill used to tell me it isn't what you go through in life that matters. It's how you come out on the other side that makes a difference.

At thirty-five years old when I first heard it, I didn't understand. Now that I am almost fifty, experienced the ups and downs of child-rearing, won and lost a few jobs, earned and spent a bunch of money, watched some people close to me fight for life and lose, well, let's just say I get it.

The cancer center where I go for treatment is one of those full service kind of places. I guess I only realized that the other day when I went for the last visit before the treatments began. I came out of the radiation side, in pretty good spirits I might add. After all, everything seems to be going my way, at least for now.

As I rounded the corner from one side of the building and looked down the corridor, I saw a very close friend sitting in a chair receiving a chemotherapy treatment. I knew she was fighting cancer. We had run into each other just a few weeks ago in Walmart.

As usual, her eyes light up at seeing me… you know, the way a friend will do; my spirits were lifted by running into her; I took ten steps down the hall, realized I was in the chemo room, and in a flash I was reminded of my mother's five year struggle with lung cancer.

I was also reminded that there are a bunch of very brave people in this world who have agreed to treatment that is often worse than the disease. I felt a little guilty because my treatment seems so easy, and my condition seems so destined to be cured.

I thought about all of that on my drive back to work, and I decided to ask you all to do me a favor. If you are a praying person, pray for people who suffer the affliction of cancer. I know times are hard, but if you have extra money, consider giving it to any organization that furthers the kind of research that may one day cure all cancers.

A few nights ago, I watched Field of Dreams for the kazzillionth time. I have no idea how many zeros there are in that number, but I am quite sure it trumps a trillion.

Of course the movie is a lot about baseball, but it is also a lot about life and all of the relationships we encounter along the way. It is about faith, and trust, and believing in things that cannot be seen or touched or explained.

One of my favorite scenes involves Ray Cancella, played by Kevin Costner, having a conversation with Archibald "Moonlight" Graham, played by Burt Lancaster.

Moonlight Graham only got to play one inning in the major leagues, and he never got to bat. Graham just knew they would send him back down to the minors, and he couldn't bear the thought of another season on the junior circuit.

So he went home to Minnesota where he became a medical doctor. He never became a major league baseball player, but he did become the kind of doctor that changed lives. Ray learned in his research about Doc Graham that he also changed a community.

In the movie, Ray offers Doc Graham the opportunity to come back to Iowa City to fulfill his dream of getting that major league at bat, and what follows is perhaps the most powerful monologue in the entire movie.

You would think I could quote it perfectly, but suffice it to say that Doc tells Ray that he would have loved to have had the opportunity to have that major league at bat...to squint at a sky so blue that it makes your eyes hurt...to connect with the ball and feel the tingle all the way down your arms...stretch a double into a triple, slide in head first, and wrap your arms around the base as if it were your child.

We think there will be other days, but sometimes today is the only day.

When Ray offers Doc his opportunity, Doc respectfully declines. He was born in this small Minnesota town; he would die in the same town, but no regrets.

Ray reminds Doc that he was a major league ball player for five minutes and that he now seems to be within an inch of his dream. Most men would consider coming that close and not realizing their dream a travesty.

Ole Doc leans in close to Ray and speaks in a whispered voice, "If I'd only been a doctor for five minutes, now that would have been a travesty."

Perhaps there will be another day to do something for people who fight cancer or to contribute to finding a cure, but just in case this is the only day, consider what you can do to fight this travesty.

The Right way to Treat People

FOR THOSE OF YOU WHO ARE keeping up with my prostate cancer progress, this past week I had the first of two High Dose Radiation treatments (HDR). I won't bore you with the details, mainly because I am not at all sure I understand how it works.

I do know that it takes four doctors to pull it off: a urologist, a radiation oncologist, an anesthesiologist, and a PhD in nuclear physics. Impressive, isn't it?

The essence of the treatment is that a high dose of radiation is actually placed into the prostate. They put you to sleep for this event, thank God, and it takes most of an afternoon to complete. By the time I realized how uncomfortable the aftermath would be, I was home asleep on the couch.

There is something to be said for quality drugs. No heroes here!

Now all of those gals down at the doctor's office have taken great pride in telling me what a piece of cake it is. Of course, none of them have had to endure the procedure, and since I have, well let me just tell you that apparently I am not the tough guy I thought I was.

Of course the day following that treatment, I went back for my regular radiation treatment. Drove myself out there…delicately, I might add. If you haven't figured it out yet, the invasive part of this procedure involves getting to the prostate from the underside of one's bottom. Needless to say, I was a little sore, and getting around was slow and easy at best.

Heck, I was so proud of myself just for getting out of bed and making it to the next treatment. The girls in the office, on the other hand, couldn't understand what the fuss was all about. They had all of these stories about men who play golf and tennis the day after their HDR procedure.

Well, let me tell you something, sister, those guys are super human or someone is lying. In fact, I told them all I couldn't believe that I had agreed to a second one of these.

Politely, they reminded me that I hadn't agreed to it at all. I am simply doing what beats the alternative.

I just want you to know that they shamed me so much that I went on to work just like any other day. I figured I'd go home at lunch, which stretched into three-o'clock, and finally a little after five, I left for home. I stood up most of the day, for obvious reasons, but I intend to make sure the new women in my life know how tough I am.

All kidding aside, the ladies who look after me at the doctor's office are all first class. They are sweet, caring, encouraging, and really know how to treat a guy…even in awkward circumstances. I am a lucky man.

Speaking of knowing how to treat people, I found something in my mailbox this past week that left me about as speechless as I can remember. In fact, when I read the letter to my wife, it was all I could do to keep from crying.

So, here is the deal. My wife, in her infinite wisdom, has been paying for us to have a cancer policy for years. Early on, I gave her a hard time for all of the money she was spending on a policy that we would most likely never use; and even in the unlikely event that one of us got cancer, we have quality health insurance which would most assuredly be enough.

Over time, I just gave up because she was determined that this was her way of helping to look after her family. As any man worth his salt knows, Mama is always right, and I have to admit it. Mama was right.

So our cancer policy has a benefit that pays upon the first diagnosis of cancer, and a few days ago we got the check. The amount of the policy will most probably cover all of the out-of-pocket expenses not covered by our health insurance.

But that was just getting what we paid for. A few days following the check, something came in the mail that was priceless.

It was a thick package that upon first inspection looked like it might be some kind of rule book. The envelope gave away the fact that it came from the insurance company, and the truth of the matter is that I opened it with some trepidation thinking this is all I need…another book of insurance mumbo jumbo to digest.

What I found inside could not have been further from the truth. The letter read as follows:

Dear Mr. Rowland:

I have just been informed of your initial claim for cancer insurance benefits. I am sorry that you have been faced with this challenge, but I sincerely hope that the financial support provided by your insurance policy will make a difference for you.

I recently became aware of the enclosed book, **Chicken Soup for the Cancer Survivor's Soul**, and thought you might appreciate the inspiring stories from those who have shared your experience.

I sincerely hope the book and your coverage through the ACME Insurance Group (not the actual company) will bring you comfort, strength, and encouragement.

With kindest regards,

…and it was signed by the president of the company…with a copy of the book just for me.

Now that is how to treat people.

Stick a Fork in Me; I'm Done!

IT WAS NEARLY FOUR MONTHS AGO when the doctor patiently informed me that I had cancer. I wrote a column shortly after that where I addressed the issue of fear. I reminded myself that for most of my life I had been either too stupid or too naive to be afraid.

But cancer is the one word in this world that can suck the air out of a hurricane, and in spite of the fact that I didn't want to admit it, the fear of a disease that kills an awful lot of people was just undeniable. In those first few days, I had a hard time closing my eyes at night perhaps out of the fear of what the next day might hold.

I am happy to report that I took my last radiation treatment yesterday, and in a weird sort of way, it was bitter sweet. Let me explain.

For the past twenty-seven consecutive business days, I have traveled to the clinic where I receive my treatments, said good morning to the lady out front who greets everyone with a smile, chatted with the nurses and technicians who have cared for me, and left happy only to return the following day for the same routine.

Regardless of the fear that comes with having cancer, the routine of these very special people becoming an integral part of my daily ritual was priceless. In a lot of ways, they are responsible for, not only my physical heath, but my emotional health as well.

That being said, I figure I owe them all a very public and heart-felt thank you.

My doctors are Bob Cowles and David Lowther. Dr. Cowles is the urologist who found my tumor, and Dr. Lowther is the radiation oncologist who mapped out the strategy for its demise. They are two really, really smart people, and they make a great team.

Of course, doctors are supposed to save people. That is what they do.

Regardless, I just wanted them to know I am grateful for their talent and compassion. It takes nerves of steel to stare death in the face, outsmart it, and take on the next case.

I know. Sometimes death wins…but not this time. I have a lot for which to be thankful, and these two guys are at the top of my list.

But the real unsung heroes of my experience are the five women who have become my daily cheerleading section for the past month. I realize they have scores of patients other than me, but you wouldn't be able to tell it by the way they act. For the thirty-minutes every day that I was in their presence, they made me feel as though I was their only concern.

Anne is the lady who sits out front and greets me every morning with a smile. She always asks about how I'm feeling, and she calls back to Leigh Ann and Lindsey to see if they are ready for me.

I learned a lot about my caregivers during our time together. Anne lives on the Hancock County side of Lake Sinclair, her husband takes her across the lake every morning by boat where she picks up her car to drive to work.

I think that is cool…actually, it is very COLD in the month of February. That's what I call dedication, no matter how much she gets paid.

Leigh Ann and Lindsey are the two radiation technicians that actually "zap" me every day. To my friends, that is how I refer to my treatments…. getting zapped.

An ultra sound, two x-rays, ten minutes of radiation to go along with conversation about our families, the weather, and how we all got to this point in our lives, and we now have a relationship with one another.

Did I mention that each day I have to strip down below the waist, put on a hospital gown with the opening in the front (thank God!), and traipse from the dressing room to the x-ray table in all my glory? They never even laughed at me once, which I find amazing because I think it is hilarious.

I told them I would miss them, but we all agreed just to meet for drinks someday. I am not interested in coming back to their domain, not even for a visit.

Leigh is the nurse who first introduced me to everything I would face over the schedule of my treatments. She is funny and a pistol ball.

She is also the person who had to field my first "sexual function" question, and given the fact that she must be fifteen to twenty years my junior, she handled it with dignity and respect. She probably laughed like a hyena when I left, but at least she didn't laugh to my face.

I got her back about a week later when, in spite of the fact that I have very good veins, she couldn't start an IV and had to hand off to Erin, her equally capable colleague. I gave her a hard time for sticking me twice and for letting Erin show her up when she found a vein on the first try.

Leigh had the last laugh, however, because Erin did such a good job that when the IV fluids hit my vein, the room spun, I got light headed, and summarily passed out. Apparently I wasn't out long, but when I came to, Leigh was fanning me with a magazine like the manager of a boxer taking a standing eight count.

Looking back on it, I think there must be something in the "Nurse Code of We Stick Together" where if you chastise one nurse, the other one gets you. Erin swears she didn't do it on purpose, but I think she slipped something into that IV just to show support for her colleague and to get even with me.

Regardless, these two women have checked on my vital signs, asked me all of the tough questions about side effects, and probably listened to much more of the details of my urinary function than they cared to know about. A good woman is hard to find!

So these five women – Anne, Leigh Anne, Lindsey, Leigh and Erin – are my new heroes, and I will miss them all. They always made me feel safe and comfortable. Every man should be so lucky!

One last thing about my cancer experience: I sometimes feel a little guilty about the fact that my treatment has been so seemingly simple and so promising for a cure. It hasn't always been easy, but I am keenly aware of the fact that not every cancer story has a happy ending.

For some reason, God has provided for me more time on this earth than perhaps I am entitled. I have no idea what He has prepared for my future, but I am absolutely convinced that it involves making every minute count.

And that is just what I intend to do.

My How Time Flies

IT IS FUNNY HOW TIME FLIES. It seems like only yesterday that I was a young father trying to eke out a living for my family. Now my kids are grown, living lives of their own and building their own futures.

Jobs have come and gone, family milestones have passed me by, and while I can't grow much hair on my head, nearly all of the hair on my face has turned gray. The tree that once stood in my front yard as a symbol of new life has grown into a nice, shade producing artifact of the anniversaries of changing seasons.

I looked in the mirror recently and noticed a few wrinkles that were not there before. My hands hurt at the end of the day mostly due to arthritis that seems to be way ahead of its time. I went to the doctor about that a few years ago, and he said I just had a good case of old age arthritis… well ahead of my time, I might add.

Mama and I were commenting just the other day about an event that was being reported on TV as being seven years old. It just didn't seem like it had been that long ago.

It's been ten years since 9/11, thirty years since I graduated from college, and almost thirty-six years since my first date in a car. I had to get the calculator out for that one.

As I write this column, I am enjoying what I consider to be the great paradox of our time. I am listening to old Larry Gatlin tunes on my Iphone. How is that for living at both ends of the spectrum?

Hold onto that thought. I'll come back to it.

A few nights ago, Mama and I attended the Relay for Life Kickoff Rally in our area. Most of you know that Relay for Life is one of the significant and visible fundraising events in most communities aimed at finding a cure for cancer.

Sponsored by the American Cancer Society, Relay for Life events are currently being planned all over our area, and if you have ever been to one, you know that these events bring out the best in both community spirit and financial commitment toward the eradication of all forms of cancer.

It seems only yesterday that being told you had cancer was a certain death sentence. When I was growing up, not many people lived long after being diagnosed. I didn't think about it much then, but we have come a long way in a relatively short time.

Next month will mark two years since I began my own battle with cancer. Add six months, and you have the time that has passed since cancer claimed the life of my mother. It just doesn't seem like it has been that long, but time flies whether you are having fun or not.

While my mother could not win her fight with cancer, my story has been much different. I am reluctant to think I have been cured, but I do know that because of the millions of dollars annually that goes into cancer research I am able to live a life today that is about as normal as it gets.

In fact, I feel a little guilty sometimes because I claim to be a cancer survivor when I know so many people who have survived under much more harrowing circumstances than I have. Other than a few side effects that are more inconvenient than life changing, my day-to-day activity really hasn't changed much.

The Relay Kickoff Rally reminded me of one of the traditions at the event in my community where each survivor introduces themselves prior to the survivor's walk and tells how long it has been since their diagnosis.

Thinking about it, I decided that this year I am not going to say how long it has been mainly because it is too much trouble for me to keep up. Instead, I intend to say it doesn't matter how long it has been because one more day is all that matters.

As Relay events begin to organize in our area, I encourage you to give of your time, talents, and gifts to ensure another successful fundraising year in the fight against cancer. In addition to the money raised to find a cure, the community spirit fostered by a common goal that unites us toward a noble cause has great power to change the potential outcome for so many victims.

With your help, a cure may be closer than you think.

Me and the Missus

For Better or Worse or Death do us Part

THIS PAST WEEK WAS ONE OF those milestone weeks in the life of the Rowland household. You guessed it. My wife and I enjoyed yet another year of marital bliss.

Now, a wedding anniversary is one of those tricky events that every man has to navigate at some point or another. We have had twenty-six of them which is pretty amazing given the current state of affairs (no pun intended) in this world.

If you count the two years we dated before we got married, twenty-six turns into twenty eight. Add the two years she knew me before our first kiss, and that makes thirty.

I hadn't thought about it in a while, but a woman who had four years to figure me out before actually tying the knot should have known better. I guess it really is true that love is blind.

I was talking to a few buddies of mine a while back, and the topic of conversation turned to how long we each had been married. We all dutifully recited the exact number of years as if our wives were secretly listening to our conversation with the proverbial dog house looming in our future for an incorrect response.

We got around to the last guy, and he sheepishly held up two fingers as if that was his final answer. "You only been married two years?" I quizzed because somehow I knew he was fudging.

"Nope. Too dang long", was his reply. I didn't laugh, not because I didn't think it was funny, but because I was afraid of the aforementioned, God-given eavesdropping capability given to every woman upon marriage with respect to the stupid stuff her husband might say.

A mental picture of our dog house flashed through my mind, and I decided it wasn't big enough for me and the dog. Besides, the dog had bigger teeth anyway, so I just kept quiet.

All kidding aside, one of my mentors in life once told me that the legacy of marriage is not so much about what you go through as it is how you come out the other side that matters. As I get older, I think I am beginning to get the picture.

It is funny how times change. In 1982 when we got married, my wife and I didn't have two nickels to rub together. I worked a job that paid $3.65 per hour, and she went to work for a temporary services agency just so we could eat peanut butter sandwiches.

We had all of these plans about how we were going to spend the first four or five years devoted to one another before having kids. The truth is that it took all the money we could make to live. Romantic frills really weren't in those early budgets.

Our honeymoon was a trip to Six Flags in a 1966 Volkswagen Beetle that had more miles on it than the speed of sound. We stayed in the Mark Twain Inn. I'll never forget it. Purple carpet on the walls. The honeymoon suit. Hey, no use holding back. Ain't nothing too good for my bride. Gas was fifty cents per gallon and that car got 30 miles per when it ran. Of course when it didn't, which was more often than not, it didn't cost me a dime. I never was quite sure which was the better deal.

Our first anniversary we went to Disney World with another couple figuring we owed ourselves something better than Six Flags. I am not sure where the entire theme park motif came from, but I guess it was the poor man's way of upgrading from economy to first class.

Now, I know what you are thinking. Surely this little trip down memory lane is not going to result in an inventory of the past twenty-five anniversary celebrations, and you would be right. I have told you about the only two I can remember. Everything else is a little bit of a blur.

I do want you to know, however, that my anniversary trip bravado did improve. There have been romantic evenings out minus the children, trips to other states, and quiet moonlight strolls through the park, holding hands, and just being together.

My favorite anniversary story, however, was the one that I think defined our relationship, both for that moment, and the future. I cannot remember which year is was, but it was well into our child rearing years.

It was a Saturday, because we had planned several yard projects to complete. We started early and worked hard. The project was probably a flowerbed or something.

The kids were playing in the yard around our feet, the day was probably sunny and warm, and our little modest home was peaceful and serene. Given the way our marriage started we had truly attained the American dream.

Later that night, we were in bed, flipping through the channels on the TV, complaining about the various aches and pains that befall one who seldom completes a menial task, when I looked at my wife and said quietly, "You know what today is?"

She had to think about it for a minute, and in a sleepy voice she replied, "Our anniversary."

"Yep."

"Well, happy anniversary, Honey."

"You, too, Baby."

Now, boys, they just don't make a woman no better than that.

How I Dodged the Valentine's Bullet

So, tomorrow is Valentine's Day, and every man worth his salt who has a significant other is either licking his chops over the fact that he has conquered the battle of the best gift ever, or he is trying to think up an explanation for why he forgot. If you are as lucky as I am, your wife will do for you what mine did for me.

Case in point.

My sister and her husband are coming for the weekend, and we are going out to a local dinner spot for a quiet meal, a live band, and some dancing. So the other night we were sitting on the couch discussing our upcoming outing when she looked at me, wrinkled her forehead with that kind of furrow that all women get when they are onto something, and she said, "We are just going out to dinner, right? No presents, right?"

I couldn't help myself. I looked right back at her with the most serious look I could muster and said, "Of course not, Baby. With the bad economy and all, just being with you will be enough."

Whew! Dodged another one.

For the past few years, however, I have taken the liberty of giving my wife the ultimate gift – her very own piece of immortality. I usually write her a letter in the newspaper.

I think about it this way. Someday, ages and ages hence, someone will be searching through archived editions of the Union Recorder looking for some really newsworthy item, and they will run across my handsome picture, be stricken by the intrigue of the headline, and be unable to stop before they have read the entire column.

There they will find the love letter I wrote to my wife for that year, and once again, I will win the award for the best Valentine's Day present ever.

I did this last year, and probably the year before. Heck, I might have even done it the year before that. I started to look back to see what I had written in previous years to be sure I didn't repeat myself, but that seemed to be a little cheesy, so I just let it pass.

Aside from the obvious benefits of writing a love letter to your wife for all of the world to see, I do this because I believe the cause of writing letters is a lost art. Also, if you really did forget to get your Valentine a present, you have all day to write a nice love letter and leave it for her to find in the morning.

Hey, you got a better idea?

So, here is my "get out of the dog house free" letter for one more year.

Dear Mama, (that's what I call her. She calls me Daddy. Don't ask me how it started; just know that it fits.)

I was counting the other day, and if you go all the way back to Ms. Florence Baxter's English 102 class in college, we've been together for nearly thirty-four years; twenty-eight officially, but I knew the first day I laid eyes on you that there was something special behind those baby blues.

And, when you opened your mouth for the first time and spouted out those first few lines of South Georgia dialect, well, let's just say I always wanted to date a woman who spoke a foreign language. I have always been captivated by the way you make the word "man" have three syllables.

I was digging through some old photos the other day, and I ran across some pictures from our wedding day. I had a lot more hair, weighed twenty pounds lighter, and looked like I'd swallowed a frog. You looked every bit as beautiful as you do today and as confident as a banker in an oil field.

You have always been the rock upon which our marriage is built, and I just wanted you to know that I noticed. Twenty-eight years later when the "c" word invaded our lives, you showed that same courage, and I love you for helping me be strong through radiation treatments, sleepless nights, and unanswered questions about the future. If you are scared, I certainly wouldn't know it.

Some people get out of bed in the morning because they love their work. Others arise because it beats the alternative. Still, others get up to no direction at all.

I get out of bed every morning because you make me go first! Just kidding.

As funny as it sounds, one of the joys in my life is to sneak out of bed on a Saturday morning, make a pot of coffee, and watch the sunrise while you sleep until well past day. When we were younger, I used to make you get up, too, but now I sort of feel like you have earned all of those late Saturday sleep-ins.

It really is funny how time changes what is important.

I know I am not always easy to talk to, and patience is not one of my virtues. I can be moody and irritable. Distant and aloof.

You, on the other hand, are always the same. I need that constant in my life, and you provide it even when I don't deserve it.

Which, by-the-way, is the definition of unconditional love, and that is what I appreciate about you most. You have loved my family, our children and me without condition. In a what's-in-it-for-me world, you never ask, "what's in it for me?"

You have been a wonderful mother to our children, and I am sure you are the singular reason for their success. On too many occasions, you had to run interference for them with a dad who was never as understanding as he should be. I hope they appreciate your sacrifice.

You have allowed me to chase my dreams, a few of which I caught...or should I say "we" caught together, and you never really complained. Too many times you have put me first, and I just wanted you to know that your selflessness has not gone unnoticed.

Oh, one last thing. Thanks for being satisfied with a love letter in the newspaper. Diamonds are really expensive this year.

All my love,
Mike

The 10K Road Race,
Kayaks, and Bicycles

WELL, IT IS THE TIME OF year when I begin my annual trek into the Mike Rowland physical fitness program. Why I do this to myself every year I'll never know.

My goal, as it is every year, is to train myself into being able to start and finish the 10K road race held in conjunction with the Dairy Festival up in Eatonton. The Dairy Festival has been going on for over fifty-years, and it celebrates our area's rich history in the dairy business.

This year's Dairy Festival will be held on Saturday, June 5, and includes all kinds of special events. My favorite part is the free chocolate ice cream sandwiches – which I usually eat five or six of to celebrate my successful crossing of the 10K finish line.

Of course, there is a slight disconnect between training for six weeks to run over six miles and then consuming mass quantities of ice cream sandwiches on race day. But, I digress.

So, I have been running – well, that is a slight over statement of what I actually do – suffice it to say, I have been jogging – okay, truth be known, maybe what I do qualifies as a really brisk walk. Regardless, I have been doing whatever it is I do for about three miles daily trying to whip myself into shape for the big race.

Race...that term actually requires some clarification. You see, the word race implies that the purpose of the event is to cross the finish line first. I suppose there will be individuals at this event that will begin with the express purpose of finishing first. My ego, however, is sufficient to sustain me through the fact that many, many individuals –both male and female - will cross the finish line ahead of me.

After all, my goal is much deeper than the self gratifying endeavor of being the winner. It is my desire simply to finish.

That's right. The race begins at 8:00 AM, and I expect to cross the finish line sometime shortly after nine. Of course, the down side of my little sixty-minute foray into sweat and pain is that a lot of people will already be deep into the free ice cream sandwiches by the time I unwrap my first.

The good news is that there will be a kazillion chocolate ice cream sandwiches available, so I will not be denied!

This year marks the third out of the last four that I will compete in the Torture Trail, as it is affectionately known. Last year, I was in Italy, but technically, that is no excuse. This year, however, is especially meaningful to me as it will be my first since turning fifty-years-old.

Now, I am here to attest to the fact that fifty is not old, but there is just something psychological about overcoming that number. Besides, I am three months past radiation treatments for prostate cancer, and all of that just makes me more determined to cross this one off my list.

For some reason, I am finding it much harder this year to get into shape. I don't know if it is my age or having my insides treated like a microwaved potato. Regardless, this has been the hardest year ever for achieving my three mile daily routine relatively pain free.

The more I think about it, my struggle has nothing to do with the cardiovascular side of physical activity. It is all of those muscles in my legs that just never seem to get over the soreness. And lately, I have endured an Achilles tendon injury which makes running down right painful.

But I am a trooper, and I want to go on record as having firmly denied that injury will keep me from competing in this year's event. I just have too much pride for that. Plus, the T-shirt is pretty cool.

Be that as it may, I do acknowledge that this may very well be my last race, not so much because I can't handle it anymore, but more because I just won't have anything to prove. Besides, all of those aches and pains I mentioned earlier are really beginning to affect my mental preparation for each race.

I am determined, however, to stay in some kind of reasonably good shape, so I have been talking to my wife for sometime about getting a bicycle. My brother-in-law is the cyclist in the family, and he has the expensive bike, the biker attire, and all of the expensive accoutrements to show for it.

I mean this guy rides forty, fifty, or even sixty miles at a time. Consequently, I consider him an expert. Personally, I don't see my behind being able to accept one of those little seats for the time necessary to travel from here to Macon, but to each his own.

So, I've been studying this bike thing for about six months. I found an outfitter nearby who seemed to have it all. I made a preliminary trip to the store, talked my plan over with their expert fitter, and within a week or so he called me to say they had just the bike for me.

My wife is a great athlete in her own right. She was a star basketball player in college, which second only to her southern accent, is what attracted me to her in the first place. At one time she could throw a softball from short to first faster than you could bat an eye, and even today she can drive a golf ball two-hundred-and-twenty yards. By the way, she is fifty-years-old, too. Sorry, Baby, but the truth was going to get out sooner or later.

Being the athletic type, she was very supportive of my endeavor to purchase a bicycle. After all, if she had a bike, too, we could cycle together. Shoot, by the end of the summer we would both be digging those old clothes out of the cardboard grave yard where all clothes that once fit but no longer do reside.

I tried to remind her of the kayaks she made me buy a couple of years ago which I think we rode in together once last year. Another thing I have discovered about turning fifty is that, at least for my wife, it has affected her hearing. She acted like she didn't hear me, and I just figured taking on a woman with such an athletic past couldn't bode well for me, so I just let it go.

To top it all off, bless hear heart, she told me she had been planning to get me a bicycle for Fathers' Day all along, which is code for "you might as well buy me one for Mothers' Day, too."

So, as of this writing, we are now a proud two bicycle family, complete with helmets, biking shorts…which by the way do nothing for my youthful figure but do come with nice padding in the seat...a must for even the novice biker...and a little computer affixed to the handlebars that tells us how far we have ridden.

So, if you see us out on the road, slow down, be kind and patient, and try not to run us off the road. Remember, we are doing this for our health. After all, where we store the bikes just isn't conducive for hanging clothes on the handlebars.

Top Ten Reasons We are Still Married

YESTERDAY MY WIFE AND I CELEBRATED our 27th wedding anniversary. I know. It is hard to believe. I still have trouble seeing myself as getting older, and it just doesn't seem possible that 27 years ago my best friend and I started down a life-long path of happiness and satisfaction.

So, I got to thinking about what actually made it possible for us to stay married all of this time. After all, longevity is a dying trait in any relationship.

That being said, I decided to develop a "Top Ten List" for why our marriage has lasted, so here goes.

Reason Ten: She is a Southerner. If you don't believe me, then just talk to her. When I met my wife in college, she was the first person I had ever known that could make the word "man" have three syllables. I just had to get to know a woman with that kind of talent, and I subsequently fell in love with the person who could turn the King's English into a foreign language.

Reason Nine: I am a Red Neck. I don't mean to be. It just happens. My wife has always kind of taken to lost causes, so trying to straighten me out became one of those challenges she just couldn't back down from. She's vowed not to leave until she is finished, so I figure we are in for 27 more anniversaries at the least.

Reason Eight: We have separate bathrooms. Now that has only been the case since the kids have moved out, but having your very own bathroom is good for at least 10 years on the longevity scale. I can throw my underwear behind the door, and she can squeeze the toothpaste tube in the middle. It just don't get no better than that.

Reason Seven: Speaking of kids, we have two sons. They are as different as night and day. She has one, and I have one. If you knew

90

them, it would not be hard to tell which is which. Having her own son has given her someone to turn to when I am being the aforementioned Red Neck referred to in Reason Nine above.

Reason Six: She loves golf. So do I. A few months after we got married, I took up the habit forming game of pasture pool. It only took one four-hour round for my new bride to question the fact that I loved golf more than her. So I did the only thing a self-respecting new husband could do. I bought her a set of clubs. Being the athlete that she is, it only took one time of hitting a seven-iron in the sweet spot, and she was hooked. We've been a twosome ever since.

Reason Five: We never go to bed mad. Well, that is not exactly true. We go to bed mad sometimes, but we have a rule about not going to sleep until we have at least settled our differences. We kiss goodnight, and we say "I love you" even if the whole not going to sleep mad thing doesn't work out.

Reason Four: Did I mention that we kiss good night, and we say "I love you" . . . even if we are mad? That way we can go to sleep. Our relationship works better when we get our sleep.

Reason Three: I let her sleep late on Saturdays. I am an early riser. I guess waking up with the roosters for more than 30 years is just a habit that I cannot break. When we were younger, I thought she had to get up when I did. After all, we might miss out on quality time together. It took me a while, but now I get up before day, quietly close the bedroom door, and watch the sun rise by myself. I've learned to appreciate the solitude, and she loves the extra sleep. Works out perfectly.

Reason Two: We have a television in every room in our house. She loves Lifetime movies. I hate Lifetime movies. She loves all those shows where they remodel homes. I hate them because they usually translate into a weekend project for me that lasts six months. We both like Andy Griffith, however, which is just enough common thread to sew us together.

And the **Number One Reason** we have been married for 27 years (drum roll please) – MY WIFE IS A SAINT. Enough said.

If I Had Only One Friend Left

LET ME GET RIGHT TO THE point. Today is my anniversary. There. I remembered, which is one of those things every man fears he will forget. Not me; not this year.

So today marks the twenty-eighth year that my lovely wife and I have been married, and by the time you read this column, we should be beginning a day on the beach at St. Simons Island – one of our favorite places to be.

In fact, I figure our Saturday will start out with breakfast at Dressner's down by the pier and then a full day on the beach. My wife loves the beach, and I love my wife. Consequently, we will be at the beach with friends to celebrate another year of wedded bliss.

Recently, we were looking through our wedding photos to help our kids find pictures they would use in the slide show for their own wedding; the entire trip around memory lane was really special. I guess the most striking thing for me was that our wedding pictures are some of the few pictures my kids have seen where I actually had hair.

Not only that, but I weighed about twenty pounds less than I do right now. Suffice it to say it has been a long time since I have seen 165 pounds.

My wife, on the other hand, is just as beautiful today as she was on June 26, 1982. And what I know now that I didn't know then is that being married to your best friend is really pretty cool.

I met my wife in Miss Florence Baxter's English 102 class at Abraham Baldwin Agricultural College, affectionately known as ABAC. We were both freshmen, and she sat right beside me in what was known then as the Business and Humanities Building.

Although we had not been properly introduced, I knew she played basketball, and having always been partial to the athletic type, I fell in love almost immediately...I just didn't realize it.

But the clincher was her Southern accent. I had heard that there were people who talked like that, but having grown up north of Perry, Georgia...which, by the way, I figure is about the Mason-Dixon Line...I had just never heard it in person.

Her ability to make every word have about three more syllables than Webster intended was...no, is...an art. There is just something about a woman who can say "maaauun" (pronounced with a long a) that is just downright sexy.

I have used this space many times to affirm the fact that my wife is a saint. Through all these years, she has put up with my goofy ideas, my weird thoughts on rearing children, and my crazy dreams. In fact, she has even chased a few with me.

We have built two houses together, a couple of sets of Adirondack Chairs, and a life that is second to none. Two adult children who represent us well, careers that have been meaningful to us, and quiet summer nights watching a full moon dance off the waters of our happy place.

We have lived in four different counties, and it hasn't always been easy. We have really never made much money, but we have always had more than we deserve. It seems like forever ago, but I can remember being one car repair bill away from not having enough money to pay the bills. If she worried about it, she never let on. She just kept the faith that we'd figure it out, and we did.

We have fought over things that mattered and a bunch of things that didn't, but we have always made up and worked things out. That's the good thing about fighting...the making up part, I mean.

We have said things we didn't mean, meant things we never said, and reached the point in our lives where we communicate best when we say nothing at all. Speaking of communicating, my wife has the habit of finishing my sentences for me. She says she does that because I often find myself speaking in half sentences, but I think it is really more a sign of how in tune she is with the way I think.

It frustrates me sometimes because she occasionally completes my sentences incorrectly...but only occasionally.

Speaking of being frustrated, I know sometimes I frustrate her for things too numerous to mention here. But she never keeps a scorecard, and she never tries to punish me. Her memory is short, but only when it comes to my shortcomings in life. She always remembers to kiss me good night before I go to sleep, and sleeping without her is getting harder and harder to do.

When we were younger, she made me fend for myself. I am sure that is because working a fulltime job and taking care of two children just wore her out. Now she fixes my ice cream without me even having to ask.

That is a special woman.

There is an old Dan Seals song that goes like this:

> I always thought you were the best
> I guess I always will.
> I always felt that we were blessed
> And I feel that way still.
> Sometimes we took the hard road
> But we always saw it through.
> If I had only one friend left
> I'd want it to be you.

Happy Anniversary, Honey! And thanks again for being my friend.

Remembering Lot and my Ice Cream Fix

MANY OF YOU WILL REMEMBER THE Biblical story from Genesis of Lot and his escape from Sodom. God intended to destroy the city with fire and brimstone because of its great wickedness. So, God sent angels to warn Lot of the impending demise of the city and the angels led Lot, his wife, and two daughters forcibly to the edge of town.

At this point, they were all instructed to flee to a neighboring town with a specific caution not to look back. Lot's wife did not follow this admonishment, and she was turned into a pillar of salt for her disobedience.

Hold onto that thought. I'll come back to it later.

So, last Monday I went for my weekly wing fix at the Brick and enjoyed a fun time with family and friends. Since I paid the bill for the family, boy child number two offered to treat Mama and me to ice cream afterwards.

Now, there are several things here worth mentioning. First, it is a rare occasion when one of the kids offers to pick up the tab. That's okay, however, because just having them around is worth the cost of a meal or two each month.

Boy number one is now in Florida, so little brother is the benefactor of my undivided attention. Regardless, I am learning that days with Dad are numbered so I am determined to enjoy every day I get.

Secondly, I never pass up ice cream…ever! The fact that it was free only added to the enjoyment.

Of course I got to thinking about the entire free thing and realized that my son was most probably paying for our ice cream bonanza with money I had given him, so free really isn't free after all. I am glad that thought never occurred to me at the time because somehow I think it would have diminished the enjoyment of the moment.

Be that as it may, we headed around the corner to Scoops for a little taste of ice cream heaven.

Now, my favorite is chocolate – hands down. No contest. I cannot think of anything more relaxing that a great big ole bowl of Breyers chocolate ice cream. When I was younger, I could eat an entire container in one sitting. I was a trained professional.

I don't know what it is about getting older, but I am just out of championship ice cream consuming shape. Actually, it's kind of depressing.

Of course, Scoops is one of those variety ice cream shops. They have every flavor known to man, and I usually venture away from my chocolate upbringing when faced with so many choices. Pralines and cream is my second choice, and since I can buy chocolate at the grocery story, I went for the caramel-pecan delicacy.

A large single scoop in a waffle cone. Doesn't that just make you want to burn the Weight Watchers manual?

I was having lunch with a few colleagues today, and one of them told the story of a dying relative who had been virtually non-responsive for a long time. Just a few days ago, he awoke long enough to request ice cream. She was fussing a little bit because the family didn't think that was a good idea. He died a few days later.

Note to family: If I am on my death bed and I request ice cream, do not deny me! Remember; chocolate first, P & C second, and then anything after that that strikes your fancy. Once I've had my way, I am really not very picky.

Now, close your eyes, and get this mental picture. We all came walking out of the ice cream shop, strolling down the sidewalk, each of us enjoying the object of our ice cream affection. My wife and I in front; my son and his girlfriend behind.

Distracted only slightly, two college co-eds came jogging by, each of them with bodies that looked like they hadn't seen an ice cream cone since their first birthday.

I could see my wife shuffle slightly as if to turn for a passing look at the youth of pique physical condition. I reached out with my left hand, stopped her before she made the complete turn, and said, "Don't do it, Honey. Remember what happened to Lot's wife?"

The Miracle of Two Ducks and the World's Greatest Grass Cutting Partner

IF YOU HAVE BEEN FOLLOWING MY column for any length of time, you will know that I retired from my job of 30 years back in April. I have played a lot of golf over the summer, cut a lot of grass, and played with Otis, my dog.

I have cooked my wife breakfast on mornings that she wanted it, washed a few loads of clothes, vacuumed the house, and loaded and unloaded the dishwasher on numerous occasions. But mostly, I have worn shorts, tee shirts, and flip flops.

What I haven't done is stress a lot over any of the aforementioned activities.

In a moment of weakness, however, I recently went back to work fulltime. Now I have to admit that this new job I have is a lot of work, but it really isn't very stressful.

Be that as it may, I got a little behind this past week, and when I came home Thursday afternoon I found my wife behind the push mower cutting our grass. Hold onto that thought; I'll come back to it.

You know, we don't talk a lot about miracles any more. Maybe it is a sign of the times and the skepticism that has been created by high unemployment, political name-calling, gridlock in Washington, our downgraded credit, and a volatile stock market.

The economy is in the tank, gas prices will never be below $2 again, and civil disagreement seems to be a thing of the past. I just think we generally don't believe miracles are possible anymore.

There are all kinds of stories about miracles. The Bible is full of them; books have been written and turned into movies that describe miraculous events. But the miracle concept just seems to have lost its luster.

On of my favorite miracle stories involves a dad who has taken his young son duck hunting. The little boy and his dad head out to the marsh on a morning so cold that there is a thin film of ice on the water.

They stand in that cold water, waist-deep with Dad blowing on his duck call trying to talk those ducks into shooting range. All of a sudden two ducks appear on the horizon, and Dad throws up his gun, levels on the ducks, and BANG, BAM, BLAM....

...and the two ducks just fly off into the distance.

The father looks at his son and says, "Son, you don't know just how lucky you are."

"What do you mean, Dad?"

"Some people live all their lives and never see a miracle like you – a little boy of six years old – have seen here today," explains his father.

"What miracle is that?" inquires the son.

"Why, the miracle of those two dead ducks flying off like that!" exclaims the father.

So I looked up the definition of a miracle. According to Dictionary. com a miracle is a noun which means:

1. An effect or extraordinary event in the physical work that surpasses all know human or natural powers and is ascribed to a supernatural cause...Let's see; yep. Fits that description.
2. Such an effect or event manifesting or considered as a work of God...Fits that, too.
3. A wonder; marvel...I did wonder what the heck had gotten into her and watching

Her struggle to push that mower with broken rear wheel drive up the hillside of our
  yard was a sight of which to marvel...

So, there you have it. Coming home to catch my wife cutting the grass because she knew I was behind the proverbial eight ball was... well...a miracle.

All kidding aside, thanks, Baby, for helping me get my ox out of the ditch. The real miracle in this story is me finding such a wonderful partner to help me with my yard work.

Vacation Time

When Life was Simple

As I WRITE MY COLUMN FOR this week I am cruising at an altitude of 37,861 feet and a speed of 490 miles per hour. I know this because the plane on which I am flying has a little screen in the back of the seat in front of me that gives just such information.

I am on my way to Denver, Colorado to catch another plane that will take me to Salt Lake City, Utah where I will hook up with my sister and her family. This is what I call a vacation.

Next week, I will be going to Missouri for two days of horseback riding in the Ozark Mountains. For a city boy, that promises to be a neat trip. I will go ahead and warn you, however, that Trudy and I are going with a couple who have been long-time friends of ours.

I sent them a copy of my article to preview because I had originally used their names. They sent me a nice e-mail back asking that I not associate them personally with my vacation endeavors.

I explained that I felt certain no one would associate their name with those pictures at the post office. Nevertheless, they insisted on anonymity. I aim to please, so I have protected their identity...for now.

Now all of this may mean little to you, but suffice it to say that anytime the four of us go off together the stories associated with our trip are unusual at best. Of course that is what makes having good friends fun. Plus, as I have mentioned previously, I need material.

For instance, there was the time we went to watch Georgia high school football games at the Georgia Dome and found ourselves needing to go up one level only to be faced with the nearest escalator that was headed in the opposite direction.

Now, I know what you are thinking. Grown people just don't do that. Wrong.

The four of us took off up the down escalator. We all made it safely, save my wife, who stumbled at the top and had to be rescued from an eventual trip back from whence she came.

Oh, one other thing I'd better tell you. I always clear telling these stories with my wife. If you have ever been married more than thirty minutes, you will understand the importance of that disclaimer.

Anyway, we all still laugh about going up the down escalator in the Georgia Dome. My friend and I thought it was hilarious from the beginning. It took our wives a few months to see the humor in our experience.

The truth is that when I travel, well, stuff just happens. I guess without the stuff, there just would not be much adventure. Trust me. Adventure is my middle name.

None of that has anything to do with this week's topic. I just thought I would give you a heads up about the weeks to come.

A couple of days ago, I was riding down the road and just happened to glance off to my right to notice a bold advertisement for an LSV. Any of you know what that is? Me neither.

I had to study it a bit, but I finally figured it out. An LSV is a Low Speed Vehicle. Up until recently we called them golf carts. I don't know when the name changed. You'd think I would notice something like that.

Just the other day I was at the golf course, and they were still called golf carts. I guess somebody forgot to tell the folks at the Uncle Remus Golf Course about the name change.

Anyway, that set me to thinking about how things have changed over the years. For instance, when I was growing up in the late 1960's and early 1970's, all the male children in my neighborhood were in competition for the lawn mowing business. The going rate was about $5 per lawn, $10 if you got to negotiate with the woman of the house.

Today, that is called a lawn service, and folks are making a good living doing what us teenagers did just for spending money. Who'd-a-thunk it?

I also remember drinking water right out of the faucet. In fact, on hot summer days after cutting that aforementioned grass, it was not uncommon to walk right over to the faucet and partake of life's essential element right out of the hose.

There was something about the rubber taste of that water that went along with the days of summer. Today, we buy water in bottles the same way we bought soft drinks back in the old days.

My Dad was born in the 1930's, and he resisted buying water in a bottle for a long time. I think it was just the principal of the thing to him. I have noticed lately that even he has given in to progress.

I also put this logic to the idea of cell phones, but I decided not to say anything more about that. The more I think about it, that topic could evolve into an entire book. In the mean time, I think I will just retreat into my memories of when life really was simpler.

Them Hills Have Eyes

I MENTIONED LAST WEEK THAT I was going to Utah to see my sister. At this writing, I am 39,000 feet above the ground on my way back to Atlanta, and I have to tell you that the trip was everything I had hoped it would be.

If you ever get the chance to see Utah, I highly recommend it. The mountains have long been my passion, and I enjoy the opportunity to visit the North Georgia variety every chance I get. But the mountains of Northern Utah are in a class all their own.

My sister and her family have been in Utah for almost four years. I have been at Christmas twice and once in the spring. The first Christmas was particularly memorable as it produced the first white Christmas my family had ever experienced. That Christmas morning, a light rain changed over to a light snow, and four days and thirty-nine inches later, I had seen more snow in one week than most southern boys see in a lifetime.

This trip results in me now having had the good fortune of experiencing all of the seasons, and I have to tell you that summer is special. The opportunity for outdoor activities is awesome. Our week was filled with golf, hiking and four-wheeling through the beautiful mountain scenery.

The most fascinating thing to me about the state of Brigham Young is the immense public access. The golf courses there rival the resort courses here, but they are all open to the public and very affordable.

I get a bit frustrated living in a geographic location that boasts perhaps the most beautiful golf courses anywhere only to find them open only to the wealthiest individuals. Oh well, that is a column for another day.

a bale of hay…with a head on it…well truth be told, he taught me to rope the bale about twice out of every ten times I threw the rope. I threw that rope a lot.

Back in my football days, I injured my right wrist in such a way as to make arthritis a constant reminder of my glory days. I didn't want to make excuses, but I figure that was the reason I never perfected that wrist movement at the top of my head that results in a cowboy encircling himself in the rope without roping himself instead of his target.

Sam tried, however, and I have to give him credit for that.

Alyssa taught me not to treat a horse like a sissy. She might have been a girl — a pretty one at that — but she was no sissy. From her I learned things like kicking a horse in the side makes her want to back up. Playing tug-of-war with the reins won't work either. And, if you want a horse to do something, then you have to treat them like children: firm enough to let them know you mean business but compassionate enough to reward them when they get it right.

I guess you could say we were paying customers, but C and Sonny just made you feel like you were part of the family. Their Christian example of love and respect was so effortless that you just had to know you were watching their everyday commitment to God's purpose.

It takes special people to open their home and meal table to complete strangers. C and Sonny are special people, and my little vacation group and I will forever be better people because of the way they touched our experience.

It may be hard to find the values of the old west in today's world of "what's in it for me", but I just wanted to say thank you to everyone at Bucks and Spurs for having us and treating us like family.

C and Sonny, if you are ever out our way I hope we can do the same.

Of the things we did, it is hard to say which was my favorite. Four wheeling up the mountain at Bear River was the most surprising. As we approached the 10,000 foot mark in elevation, reflecting back on the various creeks, wildflowers, and meadows was special.

But, nothing prepared me for the view at the top of that mountain. The truth of the matter is that I am afraid to even try to describe it. You would have to see it for yourself to understand.

Suffice it to say that the view from almost two miles above sea level of lush green vegetation surrounding a winding river meandering through the canyon was priceless.

We also hiked up Adams Canyon to a beautiful waterfall. The elevation change was about 1000 feet from the trailhead to the waterfall, and the entire event took about five hours to complete.

My wife was a real trooper. She only panicked a couple of times as we made some pretty treacherous rock crossings. She was more sure of herself going than coming. I tried to tell her them hills had eyes, but she didn't believe me. Anyway, I got several interesting pictures of her sliding down the mountain path on her behind.

I started to send those pictures along with this article, but you will remember that last week I pointed out the secret to staying married. And it does not include sending embarrassing photos of your wife's more humbling moments.

In any event, I am already looking forward to my trip to Missouri. As uneventful as this trip was I can assure you the one coming next week will be quite the opposite. As I mentioned last week, two days of horseback riding in the Ozark Mountains is sure to produce tales of suspense and intrigue.

Stay tuned.

Whatever Happened to Randolph Scott?

You know, I guess every little fella at some point dreams of being a cowboy. I'll bet every family photo album that includes kids growing up in my generation includes at least one picture of junior in full cowboy attire.

You know, the black slacks trimmed with white tassels that hung off the sides of the legs. The shirt was red, trimmed in black with those same white tassels streaming from the sleeves.

And no self-respecting cowpoke would be photographed without his trusty six-shooters hanging stately from his little hips. Top all of that off with a black felt cowboy hat that wore like the most expensive Stetson, and you have the ultimate wrangler.

Roy Rogers and Randolph Scott are images from the past, but it is still hard to beat the mental picture of the Saturday Western … cowboys riding the open range on their trusty horses with only the wind chasing their dreams. The romance of the old west represents the kind of value system that is missing in this country today.

As I mentioned last week, summer represents the height of the vacation season, and I made a decision some time ago to venture into a little taste of my aforementioned boyhood dream of the cowboy west.

Tempered with a dose of modern technology, I conducted a Google search for the ultimate cowboy vacation, and called up a friend of mine to solidify the deal. Honestly, there was no way I could have predicted the positive experience our trip became.

Now, you will remember from two weeks ago that I gave my friend the opportunity to become famous in one of my columns by sharing his identity with my reading public. In spite of the fact that I explained my

likelihood to be passed over for this year's Pulitzer Prize, he felt it best to remain anonymous. And, to this point, I have honored that request. I am still thinking about whether to violate my agreement.

This would probably be a good spot to make a long story short, but I have to tell you that five days and twenty-six hours in a vehicle just cannot be condensed into a Readers' Digest version.

Now, I have been thinking about how to slant this article since we began our ride home from Ava, Missouri. After all, I could discuss the fact that the two wives we took with us are about the most unlikely cowgirls you could imagine.

I could further embellish on the fact that the thought of spider webs, ticks, and seven hours on horseback through the foothills of the Ozark Mountains was poor competition for the outlet mall and the river walk in Branson. I could further estimate that tubing down Big Beaver Creek in the absolute middle of nowhere could never compete with fruity drinks on the beach.

Instead, I want to introduce you to Cecil and Sonny. I don't think I ever got their last names, but honestly, their sincere humility required that you get to know them on a first name basis. Cecil just goes by C for short.

C and Sonny are the proprietors of Bucks and Spurs Dude Ranch located in the beautiful Ozark Mountains of Southwest Missouri. Sonny is the voice behind the outfit and serves as the perfect cook and hostess.

C is the trail guide and the absolute picture of what a real cowboy should be. He is smart and witty and knows everything there is to know about horses. It is absolute magic to watch a master craftsman at work, and C is that and more.

He is patient and kind and willing to share his perfect knowledge with people who have to be taught the difference between a stirrup and a saddle horn. The two of them even take on interns to learn the horse and cattle business in a way that can only be taught by master craftsmen. We consequently got to know Sam, a cowboy from Italy if you can imagine that, and Alyssa, a cowgirl from Arizona who was cute as a button and held her own better than any man I ever saw.

Sam taught me to rope cows. Well, actually he taught me to rope

What I Did On My Summer Vacation

I TOLD YOU LAST WEEK THAT my wife and I were planning a three day camping trip to the mountains....in a tent. Believe it or not, the entire weekend was about as perfect as it could be.

We found the state park (thanks to our Garman Nuvi), successfully set up our tent in about an hour (no thanks to those stupid directions that come with the contraption), kayaked in the lake (my wife tipped over her kayak getting in...remind me to tell you the rest of that story some day when she is out of town.), hiked four miles up and across Blood Mountain, and made it home all in one piece.

But the entire vacation experience reminded me of a trip we took a few years ago when our kids were still in high school. What follows is the honest Injun truth of that experience, to the best of my recollection.

Now, I know what you are thinking. This is going to be one of those articles kind of like watching Uncle Albert's 8mm video film recording from his trip to the tropical rain forest. But, hang in there with me. I swear this is funny.

By the way, for those of you who are too young, I apologize for the reference to 8mm video film. For those of us old enough to remember, well, you get the picture. If you are old enough, explain it to the younger generation. In the digital video age, they should get a kick out of it.

This was one of those vacations we actually planned, and everything went as expected . . . well, almost. We started our adventure with a four-hour horseback ride through the North Georgia mountains. I have to tell you that the mountains are my passion and remarkably beautiful regardless of the time of year, but they are especially romantic atop a steady horse. Which brings me to the story.

Get the picture (to coin a Munson phrase). Each one of us received a horse appropriately named and suited for our own personality. How the guide new this is still beyond me.

I mounted Bailey first. Now Bailey was a well-mannered horse with a mind of its own, quite appropriate, I thought, given my own propensity to do things my way. My oldest child rode Jackson, an average horse who didn't make too many waves and probably isn't much trouble to raise.

My younger son rode Jackie, a mare who had a quiet spirit but was always looking for something a little on the wild side. My wife drew Duke, not particularly the brightest one of the bunch (according to our guide) which should not be compared to the relative intelligence of his rider. My wife is a smart lady. After all, she agreed to this trip.

So off we went up the mountain, and, really, everything was wonderful. The views were spectacular. The weather was perfect. Not too hot. Not too cool. We had a sack lunch at the top of the mountain where the scenery was breath-taking.

But here is the funny part. After going back down the mountain and even taking a brief run with the horses through a small meadow, I began to realize that saddles are not like Lazy Boy Recliners. And after four hours of sitting in one, places on my backside hurt where I never believed I had anything to hurt.

But at the end of the day Saturday, we were all none-the-worse for wear, and we vowed to make this an annual event. Sunday was a different story.

Aside from the horseback riding event, a major goal of this trip was to do some hiking. Sounds manly enough, right? Well, here's the deal.

After breakfast Sunday morning, we embarked on a seven mile hike up one side of the mountain upon which we were staying and down the other, an activity I had estimated to take about three hours. Oh, and by the way, there was an elevation change of about 1200 feet, a little fact I forgot to divulge to the rest of my party before we began.

Let me see if I can remember how it went. Twenty-minutes into the hike, my wife remembered some quaint little shops she had noticed on the way into town for which she was determined to visit. As fate would have it, she chose this moment to remind me of her wish.

"I gave up shopping for this?' she quipped

"But look at the view," I reminded her.

"My legs are like jelly. How long did you say this would take?"

"Don't think about that now, Honey. It will be over before you know it."

At the one hour mark, this exchange was heard: "What is this?" asked the little one about an oddly shaped object he found lying in the trail.

"Probably the bones of some poor person who tried this before," (you guess whose quote this is.)

Anyway, three hours and three bears later (sorry no Goldilocks) we stumbled back into the lodge, an opulent kind of place that was meant to far exceed the comforts of home. After an evening of gourmet food and fine wine (purely for medicinal purposes I might add), I was back in the good graces of my mate, something to be cherished since my track record is not to remain there long.

We finished the experience the following day with a lazy float down the Chattahoochee River in an inner tube. We all had separate ones, of course, which means that the "togetherness" we were supposed to experience went out the window the first time my wife got hung up in the rapids while the rest of us floated on down the river. It didn't help matters much when some little kid hollered, "SNAKE!!"

Needless to say, the end of the river float was a welcome site. The trip back to paradise was quiet. It's amazing how much you can communicate by saying nothing, and I learned, at least for this leg of the journey, that not trying to talk about it was a good strategy.

What did I do on my summer vacation you ask? I made lasting memories with my family and collected material for the book I plan to write entitled <u>Comedians Are So Funny Because Real Life Is A Hoot!</u>

The Importance of Vocabulary
in a Friendship

IT IS INTERESTING TO ME HOW, now that I am older, I have developed different friends for different activities. For instance, I play golf with the same people. I got to church with a different group of people, and I go out to dinner with yet a different set of friends.

I even have one friend whose specific job in my life is to be my adventure mate. Now, you may be somewhat unfamiliar with the term adventure mate.

After all, I will bet you have heard of soul mate and play mate and first mate, but adventure mate is probably not a part of your daily vocabulary.

By definition an adventure mate is an individual with whom one associates who, when the two said individuals are together, always results in an adventure. I have one such friend and we get together about once every two or three months just to see what kind of mischief we can incur.

Pat Schofil and I have been friends for the past ten or twelve years. Our first association began when he was selling school furniture and I was a first year high school principal. We hit it off from the beginning, and have been close friends ever since.

One of our regular activities as friends is to attend the Georgia High School Football quarterfinals at the Georgia Dome. We have been doing that for years, and the trip almost always involves our families.

Pat has a wife like mine. Mona is a saint, and probably has already earned a special place in heaven for putting up with what results when all of us get together. They also have two sons, and our kids are all close enough in age that when we get together it usually results in some of those high testosterone experiences that just really have no predictable outcome.

Our first Georgia Dome experience should have been a harbinger of events to come. It all started innocently enough when we found ourselves on the first floor of the stadium but needing to be on the second floor.

We quickly studied the situation, found no staircase in sight, and resorted to climb the only escalator we could find. Unfortunately, it was the down escalator, and we wanted to go up.

No problem. And we all just about made it, too, until my wonderful bride stumbled at the end and nearly took Mona out as she slowly grew smaller as we watched her retreat back down to the first floor.

Seven-eighths of us thought that entire experience was hilarious from the moment it happened. It has taken my wife a few years to see the humor in it. Nonetheless, Pat and I have been adventure mates ever since.

We are always looking for something to do that is just a little different. Most of the time we try to involve our wives, but they have become a little wary of our little excursions and getting them to tag along is becoming increasingly difficult - especially if the event involves animals or water.

So, Pat calls me the other day and says, "Check your calendar. How about a quick rafting trip down the Nantahala River?"

"Let me see…Okay. I'm in! What about the boys?"

"Everyone is invited. Let's take them all."

Now, all of our schedules are complicated, but we did not let that stop us. After some nifty planning and about a hundred cell phone calls, we finally assembled the entire crew at Base Camp of the Nantahala Outdoor Center.

…sounds kind of romantic, doesn't it. Base camp. The name is a bit misleading.

What we had was one small room with six bunk-style beds. Each bed had a thin mattress, and none of the windows had screens. The air temperature was about 90 degrees that day, and the one light bulb in the room attracted every bug within a hundred mile radius making opening the windows out of the question.

Does the phrase "hotter than 400 hells" mean anything to you? Well, that is about how that room felt when we all tried to go to sleep.

I don't know that I have had a more uncomfortable night of sleep in the past twenty years. My back is still stiff.

Sometime during the night, Pat couldn't take the heat anymore, and opened the windows, willing to take his chances with North Carolina mosquitoes. I know that because at six the next morning, the open window made the thunder more audible as a bolt of lightening lit up the room and shook what my number two child referred to affectionately as "the tree house".

Of course the kind folks down at the Outdoor Center were quick to point out that rafting trips do not get rained out, and we began our two-hour decent down the river in a cold, steady rain. By the way, that river water is cold, too. I don't know what glacier that stuff melted off of, but the first time we hit one of those little class two rapids and water splashed up all over me, I left my breath somewhere along the banks of the Nantahala River.

The trip was great, nobody got hurt (which is unusual), and two dads enjoying whitewater rafting with their sons was priceless. I didn't mention that Pat and Steven, my older son, tried the whole whitewater kayaking thing.

That just about ruined the "nobody got hurt" part of our trip and did result in the loss of one paddle...another story for another day.

The Adventures of Mike and Pat

MY BUDDY AND GREAT AMERICAN PAT Schofill called me about two weeks ago.

"You want to go bear hunting?" he said.

"What did you say?" I quipped. "You must have gone down in a hole because I could have sworn you said bear hunting", I replied with just enough hint of sarcasm to let him know that I thought he had been sniffing glue.

"I have not been sniffing glue, just in case you were wondering."

That is the really cool thing about great friends. You can anticipate what they are thinking just by the tone in their voice. Pat and I have been friends for a long time just in case you were wondering.

"Mona going with you?"

"You're kidding, right?

I must interject at this point the following story.

Pat and I are diehard high school football fans. Most years for the past seven or eight, we have met at the Georgia Dome to watch the high school state semi-finals, and now the state championships. We usually make it a family affair by taking our wives and kids. The highlight of the trip is usually sideline passes that we somehow finagle because Pat's dad was an important big wig in high school football in some past life.

But the defining moment in what started the first episode of the Adventures of Mike and Pat came when we all found ourselves on a particular floor of the Georgia Dome realizing that we needed to be on the floor directly above us. We looked for a stair case or up escalator in vain.

We did, however, find a down escalator, and being old football jocks ourselves, we figured making it up the down escalator would be a piece of cake. Our wives were less than thrilled about our plans to buck the system, but not being able to locate a suitable alternative, they just could not figure another way out.

So right there in the middle of the Georgia Dome, four middle-aged adults (depending on your definition of course) began to sprint up the down escalator. Honestly, I can't remember who went first, but I have a very clear memory of who went last. My wife.

The three of us made it to the top, never looking back until we had reached our goal. Trudy, bless her heart, made it to the last step or two, and I can't remember exactly what happened, but I do remember watching her travel helplessly back to the spot from whence she came – the three amigos laughing uncontrollably over the entire site of grown people acting like kids.

Trudy didn't think it was funny although she did make it to the top on her second try. Mona decided to side with her because, after all, any two women worth their salt will stick together, and that moment became the day that the loves of our lives vowed never to get involved in one of our adventures again.

So, Pat says, "Case and I went bear hunting a few weeks ago and we are going back next weekend. We plan to tent camp by the creek. We just knew you would want to go. Bring Brian if you want to"

Have you ever experienced a time when a second or two seemed like eternity? The mind is a very powerful tool, and it is amazing to me how many thoughts can go through your mind in what actually must be a split second.

While Pat awaited my response, I began to think. Let's see. A tent in the North Georgia mountains. My guess is that the air temperature will be somewhere between thirty in the morning and forty-five in the afternoon.

Along those lines, primitive camping means just that. Primitive. No running water, unless you count the creek adjacent to our campsite. No electricity. NO HEAT. Oh, I know there will be an ample camp fire, but that just can't compete with the modern convenience of a heat pump.

And what about food?

"Hey, did I mention that we are taking deer burgers and deer sausage? We will just eat what we have."

You are not helping your cause.

Look. I am a bacon and egg man. After all, I need my protein. And while I am thinking about it, God domesticated cows so we wouldn't have to eat that stuff. I guess something about the pioneer spirit just comes out in a man when he pitches a tent next to running water.

"I have my trailer loaded with fire wood. Thirty degrees really isn't that cold!"

Let me get this straight. You want me to give up seventy degree air in a warm bed with a fine woman next to me for an air mattress on the ground with the smell of campfire on every piece of cloth I will wear for the next three days?

"Ok. I'm in!" I blurted in spite of the aforementioned thinking which, as I mentioned previously, took about two seconds.

By the way, I didn't even mention it to Brian. I figure that boy is really smarter than he looks.

Now before those of you who are offended by hunting of any sort get all riled, I can assure you that I did not harm even the slightest hair of any of God's creatures. And in spite of the fact that I did carry a gun, and I did sit in the woods and enjoy the solitude of nature, rest assured that I never fired even one shot.

What I did do was enjoy two days listening to the orchestra of a running creek as the cold mountain waters of nature's purity bounced over rocks made smooth by who knows how many years of the water's travels south. And every minute that I didn't spend in the woods, I sat by a roaring fire catching up on old times with a good friend.

And the cherry on top of this chocolate trip was a light rain on Saturday morning that turned over to snow before the sun came out and turned a postcard morning into a bright, sunny afternoon. I don't know what it is about snow that brings out the kid in me, but I would drive for hours just to watch it snow for a few minutes. Get out of the car, play in the snow, and drive back home.

When our kids were little, we did it all of the time. Now, Trudy and I go on a snow drive anytime we get the chance. I suppose in a lot of ways, we are all kids at heart.

The camping trip was great. My air mattress didn't leak, and my sleeping bag was really warm. The fellowship was perfect, and at some point during the two day trip, we concocted the next episode in the Adventures of Mike and Pat.

Life just don't get no better than that.

The Beverly Hillbillies Ain't Got Nothin' on Us

MY GOOD BUDDY, GREAT AMERICAN, AND partner in crime, Pat Schofill and I, have been talking for some time about going to New York. Actually, I think it is our wives who have been putting in for the trip, but Pat and I are always in for a good adventure. We really haven't been fighting the whole New York trip thing; it's just that the opportunity hasn't presented itself. Hold onto that thought. I'll come back to it.

Recently, I was driving through the Georgia countryside on the way to an appointment, listening to Fox and Friends on my satellite radio, and just enjoying a pretty spring morning. Footnote: My oldest son thinks I am a bastion of conservative thinking. He won't just come out and say it, but he is pretty sure I am destined for cerebral ineptitude because I listen to Fox News.

I guess it is natural for our kids to believe that once their parents succumb to the half-century mark, then it is imperative upon them that they look out for us. After all, old people sometimes have trouble getting along, and our minds turn to mush from thinking only about crossword puzzles and backgammon.

He further thinks that I get my only view of the world from one news outlet, which couldn't be further from the truth; but that is a story for another day. By the way, my son and I have a great relationship, and it doesn't bother me in the least that our world view is different or that we often enjoy spirited debate over fiscal and social issues.

We are both independent thinkers, and that makes us more alike than different.

Back to my story. So I'm listening to Fox and Friends, and they advertise Fox Fan Night at Citi Field, home of the New York Mets…

121

that's a baseball team for those of you who are not sports minded…along with an opportunity to get two complimentary tickets to the game and to the Fox Fan Night pre-game party.

All it takes is an e-mail to solidify one's entry into the ticket lottery.

Now, we live in the technology-faster-than-the-speed-of-sound information age. And, since I am not far from my destination and I easily remember the e-mail address, I quickly send the e-mail from my trusty handheld device before leaving my truck for my meeting.

Then I forget about it.

A couple of weeks later, my wife and I move my youngest son's fiancé to Virginia to be near him. They will be getting married in a couple of months and moving her in the fashion and time frame we did was more a matter of convenience than anything else.

Turns out this wedding thing has turned into a story for another day as well.

The move was fairly uneventful, and Mama and I take an entire Monday to drive back home. It's about an eight-and-a-half hour drive straight through.

At about the half way mark, Mama takes over the wheel, and I think about taking a much needed nap. I refer you to my aforementioned status as over 50…a senior citizen by AARP standards…so I figure I am entitled to a mid-day nap.

Before I nap, I decide to take out my trusty little hand-held computer slash communication device and check up on a few e-mails. While I was playing cross-country mover, I have been out of touch with the e-mail world.

Now I will not bore you with all of the details of the ensuing conversation between me and Mama, but suffice it to say that I got picked to receive tickets to the Fox Fan Night experience. The only thing standing between us and Dana Perino are plane tickets, and hotel reservations.

So, using the aforementioned trusty little handheld computer slash communication device, I use the 3G highway to book two plane tickets to New York and a two night hotel stay at the Hampton Inn. The plane tickets were a little pricey, but the deal on the hotel softened the blow.

Perhaps more importantly, Mama was going to get her trip to New York.

The next day, I call my buddy, Pat, using my trusty little handheld computer slash communication device which doubles...actually triples...as a cell phone.

That conversation goes something like this:

"Pat, this is Mike. You are never going to guess what I just did."

"Let me have it."

"Trudy and I are headed to New York for the weekend to see a Mets game and take in the sights."

"You think I can get tickets on Stub Hub for the game?" he shoots back quickly.

"I wouldn't be surprised at all", is my reply.

"I just got home; let me call you back." Then he hangs up.

About two hours later, I got a text on my trusty little handheld computer slash communication device that read something like this: "Got tickets to the game. Got a room at the same hotel. Seats on the same flight. We are in!"

So Mona and Trudy got their trip to New York City, and Pat and I got credit for another one of our hair-brained, spur of the moment trips that always go down in the annals of trip lore because of some unique happenstance or snafu that occurs during the trip.

We saw the Reds hammer the Mets...an okay outcome because I am a Braves fan...the Broadway production of Phantom of the Opera, Ground Zero at the World Trade Center, the Statue of Liberty, the Empire State Building, Wall Street, Central Park, and much, much more.

We successfully navigated the infamous New York Subway system from Queens to Manhattan, and we must have walked a hundred miles. By-the-way, New Yorkers aren't really all that bad. Our treatment was superb, and we ran into a lot of please and thank you's.

Of course it doesn't hurt to be a southerner with a distinct Middle Georgia accent in the middle of Manhattan. I think New Yorkers saw that as something better than the baboon exhibit at the Zoo.

family times

All Dogs go to Heaven

SOMETHING HAPPENED TO ME EXACTLY ONE year ago this week that is worth sharing. My dog died. Now, I know how sad you must think that is, and well, actually, it is sad. But, she had lived a long and happy life. We should all be so lucky.

I knew she was in trouble by the way she was acting. My dog loved three things better than eating: riding in the back of my truck, swimming in the lake, and riding on the boat. She did all three on her last day although she barely had the strength for any of them.

When we brought her home almost ten years ago, I remember being a little nervous about having a new mouth to feed. After all, a dog is a big responsibility.

Don't get me wrong. We needed a dog...or, rather, my boys did – especially, the little one. If ever a boy needed a dog, my youngest son did, and I was happy for him. She was a chocolate lab, and we affectionately named her Katie.

As I watched the instantaneous bond that occurs when boy meets dog, I was reminded of the focus of what life is all about. As silly as it may seem, the relationship between a boy and his dog is one that begins the male trek toward the building of all other relationships . . . which might explain, generally speaking, why we are basically terrible when it comes to relationships with women . . . we are spoiled from the beginning.

Katie died on Easter Sunday. Actually, I'm pretty sure she died the Saturday night before, but it makes me feel better to think she died on Easter Sunday. That is when I found her anyway.

The same boy who needed her so desperately ten years ago grew up a little that day. He volunteered with his brother to take care of things. I am glad they did. I didn't have the heart for it.

My not-so-little-anymore boy reminded us that all dogs go to heaven, and I suppose they do. I know this: The love of a dog is hard to beat, and I miss mine terribly.

If it Ain't Broke, Don't Fix It

I RECENTLY READ WHERE THE MACON City Council passed an ordinance that limits the tethering of dogs. I guess I get that. Being a life long dog lover, I see the cruelty in putting dogs on short leashes that keep them from being able to get to food and water. It seems that was the major objective of the aforementioned ordinance.

And had they stopped there, I probably would have seen the action as just another mundane event in a world full of mundane events. But, you guessed it; they did not stop there.

The dog tethering ordinance goes so far as to make it unlawful for a dog to ride in the back of a pickup truck unless it is in an appropriate box. Now, if you have ever owned a dog that loved to ride in the back of a pickup truck, perhaps someone should have consulted the dog.

I still remember the day we brought a little chocolate lab home because I thought my kids needed a pet. My theory was, and still is, that every boy needs a dog to care for and love. A dog's love is completely unconditional and is the standard by which all little boys measure relationships which probably explains why men generally stink at grown-up relationships.

That being said, we named her Katie, and a nine year love affair began in which she warmed her way into the hearts of every family member and most other people with whom she came into contact.

My mother even loved her, which was a pretty tall order given the fact that she survived a pretty serious dog attack when getting me my first canine companion. Needless to say, she really did not care much for dogs. But, even she loved this one.

Katie was smart. In fact, she was smarter than most people I know.

And she understood me, which is more than I can say for most of the other women in my life.

She loved so many things. She loved the water. She loved walking beside the lawnmower for three-and-a-half hours while I cut grass. She loved playing fetch, and she loved getting into the neighbors' trash.

But, most of all, she loved riding in the back of my truck. I can still hear her barking as she ran from side to side across the bed of the truck speaking out to every vehicle we met on the highway.

We lived in Jesup before we moved to Eatonton. Now I have traveled every road possible between Eatonton and Jesup, and it takes three hours no matter which way you go.

Anytime we traveled from Jesup to the lake, there was a certain routine that took place, and this dog recognized the routine. She loved the lake, and she loved the trip…all three hours of it.

Once Katie realized that the lake routine was underway, she would run to the back of the truck, place her paws on the bumper, and excitedly wait for me to give her a boost into the truck bed. For the next three hours, she would ride in the back of my truck splitting her time between resting and barking at passing motorists.

Our routine was to stop at a local eating establishment in Milledgeville, pet her on the head and say a few words to her before going in to eat, and one hour later come back to the truck to find her patiently waiting for the thirty minute remainder of the trip that took her to one of her favorite places.

No matter the weather – hot, cold, wet, or dry – she loved that ride in the truck. I miss her just thinking about it. She never tried to get out, and she never acted like she was unhappy. She loved the back of that truck.

Another of her favorite things to do was to lie at my feet while I sat in the swing down by the lake. We could be sitting there in complete silence, I would say, "Katie, load up." And, that dog would jump up from a dead rest and sprint the thirty yards or so to the back of my truck, place her paws on the bumper, and wait for that familiar boost she needed to climb into the bed.

We would go to town for several hours. I might get a hair cut, go the hardware store, and stop to see a few friends. She never budged.

We could get back home, I would open the tail gate, and she might lay in the back of that truck for several hours more, not willing to take a chance that she would miss another trip to town.

I kept her in a pen for a good part of those nine years, and at the end of any given day I could tell her to "pen up", and she would respectfully meet me at the pen to be put away for the night. I am telling you, this dog was smart.

Easter Sunday was two years ago, Katie passed away. It was a sad occasion in my life. We had a hint the Saturday before that she wasn't feeling very well, but losing her was really hard for the entire family. We were all at home that day which is really unusual now that my kids are older.

The day before she died, she did the three things she loved most. She swam in the lake, she rode on the boat, and she went to town in the back of my truck. Perhaps she died of old age. After all, nine years is a long life for any dog.

I am absolutely certain, however, that had she been outlawed from riding in the back of my truck, it would have been the broken heart that killed her.

Birthdays, Vacation, and Other Odds and Ends

My little sister had a birthday this past week. I won't go into her exact age, but suffice it to say that she is not too far behind me. I may have told you this already, but she and her family have moved back to Middle Georgia from Northern Utah.

Consequently, I have only seen my sister five or six times over the past four years. I have now seen her that many times in just the past few weeks.

And, now that her children are teenagers, we have a lot more in common than we once did. She is living through places I have already been, and I have to tell you I think watching her and her husband deal with it all is about the funniest thing I have seen.

All kidding aside, they are great people, and it is good to have them back home.

So, about a week ago, my wife and I were visiting the entire clan at my sister's new house, when the subject of birthdays came up. Get the picture now; my wife and I, my sister and brother-in-law, and my parents are sitting on the deck enjoying the cooler temperatures of the late evening and relaxing with a fine glass of wine.

"Don't you have a birthday next week?" I quizzed as if I really wasn't sure.

"I do," was her quick response spoken with just enough skepticism to know I was probably up to something.

"What do you want for your birthday?" I asked.

"Why don't you get her a waffle iron? That's what you got me one year."

My wife has a memory like an elephant. I thought after fifteen years she would have forgotten. No such luck.

"But Honey, think of all those delicious waffles you cooked for the boys with that thing. That was one of those gifts that just kept on giving. By the way, whatever happened to that thing?"

"You better hope we threw it away during the last move. If I find it again, you might be wearing it."

"Awe, c'mon, Baby. Can't you take a joke?"

She gave me that look as if nothing she had heard or seen in the past decade was even the least bit funny.

"That's nothing," pointed out my sister. "I got an electric skillet one year."

And then she commenced to naming off an inventory of items that even to the untrained eye smacked of a heartless giver. My brother-in-law sat quietly hoping the moment would pass without him having to offer any explanation for his obvious gift-giving transgression.

I hate to see a guy squirm, so I offered him a life line.

"You just got a new house. How much do you want?"

Remember that "go jump" look my wife gave me earlier? Multiply that times ten.

It was becoming painfully obvious to me that my brother-in-law and I were quickly sinking into the quicksand of the marital gift-giving hell when my father unknowingly came to our rescue.

"Well, at least neither of you ever got a clock radio!" pointed out my mother emphatically. "Earl, you bought me that just so you could get up to go deer hunting."

Thanks, Dad. I thought for a minute there we were sunk.

Of course my male pride was wounded by the mere suggestion that I do not give picking out a gift for loved ones its proper place of prominence in the celestial scheme of the gift-giving galaxy. So, I resolved to make this year different.

After many hours of thoughtful consideration, I went to a local department store, picked out the prettiest gift card I could find, had the clerk put an appropriate amount of buying power on it, and mailed it to my sister. Is that special or what?

Okay, okay. So I blew the whole gift thing again. But, I get extra credit for the birthday card.

I found this really cool card that had dogs on the outside obviously preparing for a birthday celebration. On the outside the card proclaimed "Happy Birthday!" When you opened it up, it read, "From the whole muttly crew" to the tune of *Who Let The Dogs Out?*

The card cost ten bucks, but the music was priceless.

I gotta go now. My wife and I are packing for a three day camping trip in the North Georgia Mountains. I mean in a tent.

Hey, it was her idea. Well, not really, but she went along with it so I figure that at least makes her an accessory to the crime.

I checked the weather forecast, and it is supposed to rain all weekend. By the time you read this I should know for sure if Scotch Guard really works.

I hope this turns out better than the waffle iron.

Ego, Golf, and a College Education

IT'S FUNNY HOW THINGS CHANGE. WHEN I was little, my dad loved to hunt. Hunting deer was, and still is, his favorite pastime, but we generally hunted anything that was in season. He liked to fish, too, and for a long time we didn't have any other means except to fish river and creek banks.

Of course, I am his only son, and just like most fathers, I am sure my dad found the thought of he and his son sharing the outdoorsman experience as quite romantic. I am now, and was then, a dutiful son, so I went along although for my part it meant enduring waking up well before dawn and sitting perfectly still in the cold woods on the wet ground.

Or braving the hot, humid August Middle Georgia weather on a yellow fly infested creek bank where the air hung so thick you could cut it with a knife, and the occasional snake sighting kept us all on our toes.

As bad as I hate to admit it now, most of the time I went out of duty and because back in those days parents just didn't give their kids many choices. My dad said we were going hunting or fishing, and it just never occurred to me that I might say "no thanks".

Of course, now those are some of my fondest memories. I learned a lot about white tail deer, red breast bream, and chiggers. The truth of the matter is that being able to explain the rut made me quite a hit with the other kids in my neighborhood. Something about being viewed as an authority on any subject has a way of fueling one's ego.

Ego…hold onto that thought. I'll come back to it.

As I got older and had sons of my own, I understood more perfectly the romance my own father felt toward father-son outings of any kind. For some reason, I lost my passion for hunting and fishing after my kids were born, but I replaced it with a love of golf. The first time I hit a seven-iron in the sweet spot, I was hooked…have been ever since.

My boys, on the other hand, were baseball players. I was not. Don't get me wrong. I enjoy baseball like any red-blooded American male. I especially enjoyed watching my kids play.

But by the time they got old enough to play catch in the yard, my arm was worn out, and I threw more balls into the woods that they had to chase than should be allowed. I know they got frustrated with me, but their love for baseball trumped my poor athleticism for the sport.

As the kids got older, I tried to develop in them the same love of golf that enamored me, with little success. They would get frustrated to the point of tears. They were not golfers. They were baseball players, as they explained it. They hated golf.

I was crushed.

My little boy will turn twenty-one in a couple of weeks, and he called me the other day to see if I thought I might have time for a little golf after work. Please refer to the first sentence of this column. I repeat: It's funny how things change.

Of course I was able to work things out so that we could squeeze in a quick nine about mid-week. We walk, mainly because I am too cheap to rent a cart, and secondly because I need the exercise. Most of the time, Brian complains about my propensity to play the game the way it's Scottish ancestors intended, but not this day.

He had a few things on his mind, and we walked the two-and-a-half miles or so talking about growing up, the future, and what kind of next steps there might be for both of us. The golf was really secondary to spending time searching for all of the answers to the questions of life.

He is trying to figure out what he wants to be when he grows up, and well, quite frankly, so am I. He reminds me so much of me when I was his age, that I just have to smile thinking about it. He wants to be grown, but growing up scares him to death. He seldom enters a venture without a buddy, and the thought of being alone worries him. I can identify with that, too.

So we tee it up on number nine, and he begins to tell me about something he learned in his ethics class in college. I didn't know they taught ethics in college, but I am encouraged to know they do. I can use all of the help I can get.

He summarily launches into a monologue about psychological egoism. Psycho what? Psychological egoism. Whatever happened to good old fashioned algebra?

Turns out that psychological egoism is the view that humans are always motivated in their actions by self-interest. Even in what seems to be acts of altruism or benevolence. It claims that when people choose to help others, they do so ultimately because of the benefits they expect to obtain, directly or indirectly, for doing so.

Deep isn't it?

Brian said when he thought about it, the entire thing made a lot of sense to him. I, on the other hand, tried not to think about it. After all, I needed a good tee shot on number nine so that I might be motivated to play again sometime…even if, technically, there isn't really anything in it for me.

But now that I think about it, there may really be something to this pshcyobabble egoisticism thing…or however you say it.

It seems that my son needed a little fatherly advice from me, and what I got from him was that father-son golf outing that seemed so elusive when he was little. Seems like a fair trade to me even if it was motivated by our self interests.

What'll they think of next?

Memories That Make You Smile

It was nice to see a little sunshine this week after almost fifteen inches of rain at my house. For a while there, I thought I was going to have to use some of my scrap lumber to build a very big boat and dust off my old math book that reviews cubits as a unit of measure.

I was driving home from work last week, tapping my fingers on the steering wheel to the sound of some really good bluegrass music, and day dreaming about a topic for this week's column. And without even realizing it, a big grin broke out across my face.

It was a memory from my childhood that made me smile.

In 1966, my father bought the only new vehicle I ever witnessed him purchase until well after I had married and left home. It was a Volkswagen Beetle, and I can still remember the salesman at the dealership pushing it out of the showroom so we could drive it home.

I was six-years-old that year. It's funny what you remember.

It was kind of a weird blue color. Not exactly blue, per se, but more of what turquoise might look like if it were way too dark.

I think it is worth mentioning that a Volkswagen "Bug" as it was affectionately called was not the most popular auto on the market. In fact, it was kind of a novelty. It sounded like a souped up sewing machine and had two-sixty air conditioning - two windows down at sixty miles per hour. Come to think of it, most people who encountered the undersized import gave you that look as if unable to believe any sane human being would actually be seen in public behind the wheel.

That car became mine in 1976 when I turned sixteen. I drove it until I finally traded it in 1983 for my first pick-up truck. At some point during my teenage years, my uncle painted it for me. Metalic blue. There was no other Bug like it.

About ten years ago, in Savannah, I saw an exact replica of my first, four-wheeled love. It was metallic blue and restored perfectly. I couldn't help but look in the windows, and it had all of the original knobs and buttons. The upholstery was even vintage.

I almost cried.

There were a lot of good memories in that car. My dad taught me how to hunt and how to drive at the same time – both by using that car.

While a lot of father son duos went to the golf course on Sunday afternoon, my dad took me to the woods. I was about twelve, and as you might imagine, there are a lot of other things for a twelve year old to covet on a Sunday afternoon.

But my dad was pretty smart. Shortly after we pulled off of I-75, he would stop at a little convenience store, buy him a chew of Red Man, and let me drive the rest of the way to our favorite hunting spot. Looking back on it, that was pretty cool.

That little car got me through three years of high school, four years of college, and one year of marriage. She had 180,000 miles on her when I let her go. Unheard of for those times. The speedometer had been broken twice, so we really do know how far she had gone.

But the memory that made me smile involved the time my parents decided to load up my sister and me for a trip to Washington D.C. 575 miles one way. In the heat of summer. With no AC in a car about the size of a pack of gum.

I have been trying to remember what year it was. I must have been about eight-years-old because I think my sister would have been four or five. I do remember this: somewhere on the God forsaken path between here and there, my sister and I got into one hellashus fuss.

I couldn't tell you the details if I had to, but this much I know. Somewhere in all of that fussing and fighting, a five-year-old little girl kicked me in the nose with those black, hard-soled, patent leather shoes that were the rage during the Sixties.

Now, I don't know if you have really given any thought to what happens when the aforementioned shoes meet the soft, flesh tissue of an eight-year-old's nose, but suffice it to say that I bled like a stuck pig.

The rest of the trip is a blur, but I don't remember getting much sympathy from the front seat. The truth is that I probably got what I deserved.

I tell you that story to tell you this story. In about a week or so, my sister and I will take my father to Washington D.C. to see his ailing brother. It will be a pilgrimage of sorts because it will be the first family trip we will have taken without my mother.

She passed away a couple of months ago, and I know she would have enjoyed the thought of me and my sister riding in the backseat on the hope that another fight might have broken out between competitive siblings.

I'd hate to disappoint her, but we are all grown up now…well sorta…but I think I will make my sister drive and wear tennis shoes. Just in case.

Parenting, Homemade Biscuits, and the Empty Nest

My wife and I are experiencing the empty nest at our house. Now, let me be clear. In spite of the fact that this glorious happening has been our experience for a couple of years now, it suddenly feels different.

Don't get me wrong. I love my children as much as the next guy, but I'll have to admit that there was something liberating about not having to keep up with their schedules.

I quit worrying about when baseball practice was over, who the latest girlfriend was, and what time they were coming in at night. After all, since they were both out of town, what could I do? Which is something I have been working on...not worrying about things I cannot control.

Truth be told, they both lived just down the road twenty minutes or so, and somehow that just didn't qualify as long distance. If I needed them, they were close enough. When I'd had enough, I could send them home.

Occasionally, when we really missed them, their mother would invite them for supper. They almost always brought friends, and I got a circus side show kind of excitement out of watching college-age kids devour a pan of Mama's homemade biscuits.

When it comes to eating, both of my boys are trained professionals. And they hang out with friends who have similar credentials.

As a little side note, my mother tried to teach my wife the art of homemade biscuits from the time we started dating. In the early years, well, let's just say that I ate a lot of biscuits that tasted okay, but they usually looked like a cross between a large high school spit wad and a hockey puck.

I can say that now, lovingly, because my lovely bride eventually mastered, not only the art of tasty biscuits, but she can now make them look just like Mama did. Every man's dream. A wife that can cook like his Mama.

Before she died, we even got my mother to admit that her favorite daughter-in-law had at least equaled her in the Pillsbury Bake Off homemade biscuit taste and look alike test. That was a kind of monumental accomplishment because my mother seldom bestowed such an honor on anyone.

This past July, however, my older son left home perhaps for good. He and his fiancé are graduate students at Florida State University, and something about having one of your children cross a state line, establish residency, and carry an out-of-state driver's license has a sobering effect.

For the father of sons, I cannot think of a prouder moment than that of seeing your child make it on his own. Of course he is not officially off the payroll, but he is actually getting paid to go to school which reduced the required local effort out of Dad's checkbook. The economy being what it is, getting one of my kids on his own may be the closest thing to a pay raise I see for awhile.

Any father even worth half his salt places most of his fatherly effort into producing the kind of young man who can acquire a job, keep it long enough to qualify for benefits like sick leave and health insurance, and eventually serve as the qualified leader of a family of his own. If he's lucky, Junior never has to come home because he is lost, homeless, or broke.

It is a proud moment when a father realizes that all of the training, all of the lectures, and all of the sleepless nights have led to financial and social independence. After all, that's what it is all about.

So the kids have been in Florida for about two months now, and Trudy and I decided to make our first trip down to see them. They really are cool kids, and we miss them terribly.

We had a nice visit. Steven and I played golf at the FSU course, which was really cool, and Meghan and Trudy went shopping. We took them out to a fancy restaurant, I paid the bill, and there was something satisfying about following in my own father's footsteps.

These kids are so smart and so goal oriented that it is scary. As much as they enjoyed having us around, I knew they had a lot of school work to do. Sometimes you just know when it is time to leave, so shortly before lunch on Sunday, Trudy and I packed up, said our goodbyes, and headed north.

The drive home is a long one. It probably takes four hours straight through. We made a couple of stops along the way, and the trip home took most of the remainder of the afternoon. And the entire time something was bugging me.

Sometime Monday, it hit me. In spite of the fact that a wedding is three seasons away, I consider Meghan as much my own as her betrothed. After spending the weekend with them, it was obvious to me that they are well on their way to making a life for themselves.

They have their own schedule, their own ideas, and their own way of doing things. They are simple, grounded, and smart. They are fiscally conservative, not overly enamored with possessions, and practical.

They are making a world for themselves and at the same time it was exciting and sad. I cannot describe the pride that comes with knowing that someone you have loved all of his life is going to be okay.

And at the same time, my own life has changed forever. I am really not sure how I feel about that, but I think I am beginning to understand my own parents a little better.

Summon Your Courage
Courtesy of the Internet

I MENTIONED LAST WEEK THAT SUNDAY was our first Mothers Day without my mom. She died last summer after a long battle with cancer, but we all had a nice visit down at my sister's house.

My dad wrote my sister and me a nice note for Mothers Day. It was a little unexpected, but only a little. I did not commit his comments to memory, but suffice it to say that he wanted to make sure we both recognized our mother's impact and contribution to our success. It was a sweet note, and I think I speak for my sister when I say that it was not unappreciated.

It is true that in most ways we are all different. We come in all shapes and sizes; in different colors and hair styles. In fact, some of us have hair and others do not. Personally, I do not find the latter part of that statement particularly funny, but a lot of my friends do.

Some sense of humor.

Some of us are tall, and others are short; skinny and fat; some of us even look like our pets while others can't stand the thought of having a pet.

Yet even in our uniqueness, there are so many ways in which we are the same. All of us experience the physical pain of injuries to our bodies and the emotional pain of injuries to our souls. We all aspire to greatness even if greatness seems elusive.

We all have an inner strength that surpasses even what we think we are able to bear, and yet we are as fragile as the first flower of spring. And it is this sameness that unites our humanity even when the way we view the world can be so different.

Because of that dichotomy between what makes us different and similar, I believe we all possess two sides, and my mother was no different.

On the one hand, she could be the most demanding human being I have ever known. On the other hand, she couldn't bear to see her family hurt or struggle.

The benefit for my sister and me is that I think we learned from both of her sides. There were some things she would do that we learned to emulate. Others we determined wouldn't be our way. I suspect that is true for most parents and children.

But no matter how hard we try to deny it, we are both our mother's children. And for all of her faults, I am especially aware today of all that she taught me about how to be a responsible, caring adult. I just didn't want there to be any doubt that I know from whence my upbringing came.

Yesterday, my little boy turned twenty-one. Now, I am not exactly sure what that means. Oh, I suppose I get the usual things like being legal and having the last laugh when the dude behind the bar asks for your ID because he is certain you look more like a kid than an adult.

But, I am not at all sure how I feel about knowing that time marches on, and I really am on the backside of my better years. I also know that my son is at one of those crossroads in his life where he has to make the next move, and whatever move he makes will likely shape his future for years to come.

Life just doesn't seem as easy as it was when I was growing up. It seems to me that kids have more and fewer choices at the same time, if that makes any sense. The strategic importance of their next move in a world with such economic uncertainty frightens me. I can only imagine that it scares the devil out of them.

And yet the truth of the matter is that this generation is better prepared than any other to live in a world that is remarkably different than the one I found at twenty-one years of age, which by the way was twenty-nine years ago.

Think about it. If I were writing this column twenty-nine years ago, I would be typing it on an IBM Selectric II electric typewriter. If I were lucky, it would have an automatic correction ribbon. If an electric typewriter wasn't available, then that would be okay. After all, I learned to type on a manual.

When I finished my work, I would have to hand deliver it to the paper or send it through the mail. I "wrote" this column on an IBM Think Pad personal computer while sitting on my porch, watching the dog play, with a power source that is battery supplied and lasts four hours.

When I get ready to share my intellectual capital with the newspaper, I will link to the Internet, via a wireless access point, log into my e-mail, and in a matter of seconds, my little masterpiece will be sitting in Vic Powell's inbox waiting to be edited for publication.

Amazing, isn't it?

And this is the world in which our kids find themselves. A lot of the jobs today that require technical experience more closely resemble video games than anything we all did when we entered the workforce. The way information is received and transmitted is like something out of Star Trek compared to the communication tools with which my generation functioned.

There is a lot of bad news out there, and the main reason we know about it is that we can receive it all instantly. Think about it. A century-and-a-half ago, news of an oil well off the Gulf Coast (if there had been one) spewing millions of gallons of oil into the ocean may never have reached the East Coast.

Oh, I know the world was just as complicated then as it is now, but we just didn't know about it. I guess ignorance really can be bliss.

So, just like any responsible parent, I worry about my little namesake. What I want for him as he passes into adulthood is really very simple: happiness. On the outside chance that he will read the newspaper on a Saturday morning after becoming legal, I leave him with this simple thought:

If you summon your courage to challenge something, you'll never be left with regret. How sad it is to spend your life wishing, "If only I'd had a little more courage." Whatever the outcome may be, the important thing is to step forward on the path that you believe is right.

Just so you know, I got this quote from the Internet.

The Case of the Missing Flag

I HAVE BEEN WRITING THIS COLUMN for somewhere in the neighborhood of five years now, and thus far, I have included as a target just about everyone in my immediate circle of influence. I have written about my sister and her family, my father, my wife, my mother, my children, my dog, and a few of my close friends.

In fact, I recently had a frequent dinner guest implore me to write something about her in one of my columns. Of course everyone else at the table who had found themselves the subject of my newspaper prowess cautioned her in a unified voice to be careful of that for which one asks.

That hurt. Everything I write about is true, based on fact, or could have happened. That sounds fair to me.

I have discovered, however, that my in-laws have escaped any notable reference in any of my work, and it is with great pride that I set out in this column to correct that travesty.

Let me first say that my in-laws are wonderful people. After all, they have put up with me and my feeble attempts to look after their daughter for over thirty years. As with any relationship, ours has not been without some trying moments, the most notable of which being the day I whisked their daughter away from the friendly confines of South Georgia.

Be that as it may, they have tolerated my dragging their only child from the four corners of the state, and I will always be indebted to them for trusting me with their offspring.

So a few days ago, my mother-in-law calls to tell us that someone has stolen their United States Navy flag right out from under the little carport that sits adjacent to their house. My wife bought them that flag in honor of their grandchild's induction into the Navy.

Of course I am listening to a one-way conversation from my wife's end of the phone, but I am immediately reminded of my favorite one liner from Larry the Cable Guy: "You believe that?"

Now, I will have to admit that my first inclination was to invoke the goofy rule, but I resisted the temptation to do so. For clarification, the goofy rule goes something like this: If it sounds goofy, then it probably is.

Why would someone steal a flag from under your carport without taking anything else of real value? Sounds goofy, doesn't it? See how it works? By the way, you now have my permission to use the rule anytime you need to.

I didn't say anything, but I did recommend to my wife that her parents make a police report because if someone in Podunk South Georgia is going around stealing flags, then the police should know.

By the way, I looked up Podunk via the Internet, and the evolution of the word is a little complicated but suffice it to say it refers to plain honest people as opposed to more sophisticated ones with questionable values. That describes my in-laws and where they live perfectly.

Now, it took about twenty minutes for my mother-in-law to call back with the news that my father-in-law had located the flag in a location subsequently different to the aforementioned carport and that the flag was not stolen after all; just misplaced.

There you go. Mystery solved; case closed.

Except I got to thinking about the symbolism of what had just happened, and I wish that I could say that something similar had never happened to me. In fact, I would venture to say that most of us have fallen victim to misplacing something of value or importance only to cover up our own accountability by blaming its disappearance on the more dastardly forces of the universe.

I wonder why that is? And what does that really mean for how we hold ourselves responsible in our families, our work, or in our relationships?

I wish I had answers to those questions, but unfortunately, I do not. What I do know is that perhaps it is human nature to believe the worst first – you know, a kind of expect the worst but hope for the best mentality.

Or perhaps it is human nature to dodge the role each of us plays in controlling the outcome of our actions or events that affect us negatively. I can think of very few times that I have experienced adversity in my life when at least some of the blame didn't belong to me.

Or even still, maybe it has more to do with the way we jump to conclusions without all of the facts only to find out that our incomplete information takes us down a path that never proceeds to its intended destination. You give me good information, and I can make great decisions. You give me poor or incomplete information, and I can mess it up as well as anyone.

Or maybe – just maybe – experiences like this one are intended to make us look into our own actions with the kind of discriminating eye that just might bring about change.

All of that from a missing flag.

You Just Can't Beat the Love of a Good Dog

WELL, IT HAS HAPPENED. I TRIED to avoid it as long as I could, but I finally gave in. I have joined the millions of people across the world engaged in social networking via cyberspace.

That's right. I am now on Facebook.

For those of you who have had your head in the proverbial cyberspace sand, Facebook is where you can go to network with friends, loved ones, colleagues, and just anybody in general from your computer. If you are my age and you have trouble with this concept then find any twelve-year-old to assist you. You will be an expert in no time.

I bring up Facebook for two reasons. Number one: If you are the parent of a child who spends a lot of time on the Internet, then I recommend you open up you own Facebook account, ask your child to make you a friend, and visit his or her Facebook page often.

Wait a minute. I said ask your child to make you a friend. I retract that statement. Make that a condition of your child being allowed to use the computer at home. They will balk at first, but tell them that having you as a friend is just the cost of doing business.

Look, when it comes to raising children, you just cannot let them play by themselves in their own sandbox. Get in there with them. It may be a little dirty at first, but your kids will appreciate you setting their social networking parameters and establishing some boundaries.

And number two: social networking is really pretty cool, and I think I am having more fun at it than the kids. I have stayed in touch with some old friends and made a bunch of new ones.

Case in point: My good friend Robin from another city and another time entered a post (that's what you call it when you write something on your Facebook wall...see you learn something new every day) announcing that her female lab-mix dog had puppies a week or two ago.

Now, we had a chocolate lab in our family for nine years. Katie died about two years ago, and my wife and I miss her terribly. As much as we miss her, however, we had both decided that we would not have another dog because we just seem too busy. It just didn't seem fair to take on another mouth to feed when we don't seem to have enough time for all of the other mouths we are responsible for feeding from time to time.

The younger of those mouths came out to the house a couple of weeks ago, and brought with him his girl friend and her dog. The dog is a lab-bulldog mix...imagine that...but he was cute as a button.

Of course that was kind of like holding someone else's baby, and I could see the look in Mama's eyes. So, when Robin offered up her puppies for adoption, I just could not help myself.

So, with the help of Facebook, I have reserved the prettiest, chocolate male of the bunch. I figure around Thanksgiving we should be getting our new little bundle of joy. I can hardly wait.

Of course every dog has to have a name, and Trudy and I were running down the list of potentials the other day. Let's see...Chuck... no, that doesn't sound right...How about Luther? That just doesn't roll off the tongue. We've had a Charlie, and Spot just reminds of the "See Jane run " days, so we nixed those.

How about Earnest T. Bass? Nah....too long and Earnest by itself just doesn't befit a dog. Andy? Nope. Opie? Too corney.

How about Otis? Otis...I like it! Otis the dog...has a nice ring to it I think.

So, thanks to Facebook, social networking, and my friend Robin, we will soon have a little chocolate lab puppy named Otis. I'm looking forward to having a new tagalong. You just can't beat the love of a good dog.

Whew! That was Close

My wife and I are living proof that the human memory is shorter than the half-life of Roentgenium, formerly known as Unununium. No, this is not a typographical error, but it is my attempt to capitalize on the large amount of money I spent on Boy Number One's college education.

Roentgenium is number 111 on the periodic table due to its atomic number. This according to my chemistry educated son.

I vaguely remember atomic number from my high school and college chemistry days. I actually even remember the term half life and that it is short. Don't ask me for any more.

This is about as much research as you will get in any one of my columns. Preparation was never one of my strong suits.

By the way, in case you are wondering exactly how long the half life of Roentgenium is, you will just have to Google it. After all, if I tell you everything, how will you ever learn?

Remember that one? I digress, which seems to be happening to me more and more as I get older.

Case in point. My bride and I recently decided to re-enter the pet world; specifically, we are now the proud parents of a cute little ball of fur that is part lab and part something else.

If you didn't know better, you would swear he is a grizzly bear cub. Come to think of it, the way he chews on everything, I am beginning to believe that there are things the previous owner didn't tell us.

The truth of the matter is that he is just a chocolate lab puppy, and we have absolutely fallen head over heels in love.

Now I have had dogs in one form or another all of my life. My first dog was named Spot, mainly because he was white with black spots. We had a Buddy, and a Lady, and a Kate and a Charlie. Kate and Charlie we had at the same time. Having two dogs is worse than having two children. Hold on to that thought…I will come back to it later.

Since my kids were born, we have had a Peaches, a Henry, a Zeb, and a Jo- Jo. And, of course, we had Katie. She died of old age about three years ago, and we have missed her ever since.

Our lives are complicated, however, and Mama and I had vowed not to get into the dog business again until we retire. Since I have recently learned that life can really be too short, we changed our minds, and now we have taken the whining-puppy-in-the-middle-of-the-night plunge.

We have named our new bundle of joy Otis in honor of Otis Campbell of Andy Griffith fame. Otis Campbell was the town drunk but that has no connection with why we chose the name. We just thought it had a nice ring to it.

Just so you know, I did not bring Otis home alone. A buddy of mine was looking to surprise his wife with a new puppy because she recently ran over one of their dogs with her car. The dog had to be euthanized, and so my friend just thought his wife would appreciate a replacement puppy.

I'm not sure how that has worked out, but I am absolutely sure that the Rowland's are not a two dog family. I got him a girl, and we didn't have a name for her so we just called her Sister.

Let me also be clear that we have always had outside dogs, and Otis doesn't know it yet, but he will be no different. I say he doesn't know it yet because he has spent the night in the house every night since he joined the family.

The first night, the two puppies were so cute when we laid them down for bedtime…until about 12:30 AM when they decided to play a game of chase around our bedroom. It's amazing how much noise those two little rascals could make.

We finally got them back to sleep…until about 3:00 AM that is, when their natural bodily functions took over. In case you are wondering, that is code for they had to pee and poop.

Needless to say, after two hours of sleep, my wife said, "Those dogs are sleeping outside tonight."

"Aw, 'comon, Baby. They are just puppies. Besides, if we put them in their little pen under the carport, they will start whining and crying at about 3:00 AM anyway. You will listen to it for about five minutes, and then you will make me go outside, in the cold, and bring them in anyway. So, why don't we just save me the trouble of having to go outside in the cold at 3:00 AM?"

Night number two wasn't quite so bad, because Sister went home to her new family earlier that day. My buddy said, "If I get in trouble with my wife, can I bring her back?"

"Nice try", I said with a convincing look. "Don't you bring that dog back."

I sent my wife an e-mail to let her know that Sister would be gone when she got home, but not to worry. She sent me one back saying something about how much she missed Sister even though she didn't think she would.

I dodged that little episode of hormonal weakness by explaining to my spouse that every good dog needs the undivided attention of his or her master. She bought it as evidenced by the return message I got which was "Sounds good."

Whew…that was close.

Everybody we know on Facebook just loves our little puppy. We posted pictures to celebrate our new arrival, and all my "friends" can now see the little fur ball that stole my heart. By the way, if you guys were real friends, you would take a night occasionally.

I know. Nice try. You can't blame a guy for trying.

By the way, on the prostate cancer front, I got a great report from my CT scan. I am the picture of health except for my prostate. No cancer anywhere else. I do have a gall stone. Go figure?

The doctor said we wouldn't worry about that right now. Hey, he is the genius.

I still need to have an MRI so the doctor can decide just how to proceed with treatment, and that happens in early December. Otherwise, the entire road to a cure sounds more like a piece of cake every day.

Bacon and Egg Sandwiches, a Dirty Old Egg Sucking Dog, and Memories of my Mother

As I GET OLDER, IT IS the simple things in life that satisfy me most. I recently re-discovered this one Saturday morning after a particularly hectic week at work.

In order to set the stage for this experience, let me rewind the clock some thirty-eight years or so. My dad first started bringing me to Lake Sinclair when I was about twelve.

Our first boat was a fourteen-foot , aluminum boat with a 20-horsepower Johnson Sea Horse motor. We used to put in over at Haslem's Marina and fish one of our two favorite places. The first was a little creek somewhere near Optimist Island, the location of which I would be hard pressed to find today. Often, we would start there, and finish the day at our second favorite spot – tied to the railroad tressle at the marina.

At the time, I probably saw fishing with my dad as a minor inconvenience. Today I wouldn't give a million dollars for the memories.

For me, I went for the opportunity to drive the boat. I now know that he must have gone to steal a chew of Red Man and to get away from the stress of being the breadwinner for his family. I am sure he enjoyed my company, too, but at my age, I now understand the stress thing.

The important point of this story is that my dad introduced me to what has become a life-long love affair with the lake. Sometime during my high school years, my parents managed to scrape together enough money and courage to buy a piece of dirt with a hundred feet of shoreline, and the first time I ever saw it, I was hooked.

The lake has been my special place ever since. By the way, last week I parted with that old boat and motor. It had been sitting in my yard for years, and I finally found it a good home with someone who, I'm sure, will take good care of it

For many years, our lake experience consisted of a drive way from the road, a cleared off spot down by the water, and a large wooden spool, the variety of which is used to house electrical wire prior to finding its final resting place atop a power pole.

We camped in those early days, and I will not bore you with those details because to be honest with you, I have forgotten most of them. The one thing I do remember, however, is that my mother could cook a full gourmet meal from a Coleman stove sitting atop that old wooden spool.

I can smell the bacon cooking just thinking about one of those early morning breakfasts. I even remember the time she cooked perfect Southern fried chicken with rice and homemade gravy to boot, all from an iron skillet that we still use today.

Those were some great memories.

We have come a long way since then. A house now stands where most of those memories took place. A maple tree has taken the place of the old wooden spool, and we have traded that old Coleman stove for a gas grill with a side burner.

Now, I have been awaking each morning at 5:30 for as long as I can remember. Because of that habit, my biological clock does not discern between Saturdays and Sundays. Consequently, my weekend routine is to wake up well ahead of my wife, drink two cups of coffee, while she stumbles out of bed – usually around 8:00.

As often as our schedule permits, I then cook bacon and egg sandwiches on the gas grill. Sizzling bacon just smells better in the outdoor air than any other place I know. It reminds me of those camping days. Most Saturdays, Trudy and I just eat them is silence while we relax by the water. Of course I now cook one extra egg and a couple of extra pieces of bacon for our chocolate lab, Otis.

Just so you know, Otis likes his bread toasted lightly on one side only.

Last week, we marked the one year anniversary of my mother losing her fight with cancer. I knew it was coming, and actually had time to think about it. I called my dad just to see how he was getting along, and he really seemed just fine. The day came and went, and I guess life got in the way of a whole lot of sentimentality.

By the time you read this, however, depending on your weekend schedule, I will be enjoying the smell of cooking bacon, sipping on my morning cup of coffee, and settling in for Otis to make his weekly run at stealing the bacon before I finish the eggs.

My mother would have enjoyed that. She never cared much for my dogs, but she sure liked camp style cooking. And she may have loved the lake just as much as I do.

Born to Swim and Another Year Goes By

MY CRAZY, TWO-BY-FOUR EATING, BIG GAL lute of a chocolate lab is even more dysfunctional than I first believed. By the way, I looked up "big gal lute" on the Internet and found that the term is Scottish slang for a clumsy person or one of limited intelligence.

OH MY GOSH! Otis is not a human, of course, but that definition suites him perfectly. He is as clumsy as if he had four left feet, and his intelligence…well, let's just say that he has graduated from chewing wood products to lava rocks.

If I'm lying I'm dying!

I recently put lava rocks into my landscape, and it took him about two seconds to chew one right down into his digestive tract. I don't even want to contemplate how that is going to turn out – no pun intended.

But, I love him dearly. His favorite new game is to come into the house, run upstairs, find one of the socks I threw close to the clothes hamper, and take it downstairs to show Trudy what a slob I can be.

Traitor!

I have tried to teach him that us men have to stick together, to no avail. He is a pushover for two bite-sized dog biscuits and a quick rub behind the ears. The last human to pull that off is the new object of his affection.

Even still, he is my hero.

Oh, I almost forgot. This past weekend was beautiful, except for the lightening show Sunday night, and we spent most of our time doing all of that yard work that piles up over the winter. Ole Otis spent the entire two days tagging along and just getting into general mischief.

And that's how I discovered it. The goofy dog cannot swim!

No kidding! As God is my witness, a dog that was carved from a breed that is born to swim just can't do it.

Don't get me wrong. He loves the water. And it's not so much that he can't swim as it is that he absolutely does not know how. You would just have to see it to believe it.

He wades down the boat ramp to about shoulder height, and at that point, just as if he were a small child, he carefully reaches out with one paw to find the bottom. If he can touch it, he takes another step. If he can't, then he turns back.

He did misstep at one point, and absolutely fell in. Instead of dog paddling, he started slapping at the water as if he were a drowning beach go-er! He had the water frothed up in a frenzy, and he looked like he was trying to perfect the Australian crawl instead of the dog paddle.

And then it happened.

The poor little fella lost his footing, stumbled, and plunged his entire oversized head into the water. I mean he took a nose dive, his entire head submerged in the stained water of Lake Sinclair.

Mama and I were rolling on the ground in hysterical laughter. I am telling you, it was the stuff Funniest Home Videos is made of!

I can't help but chuckle a bit just thinking about it.

For all of his antics, however, he is a hoot. I can't imagine what I did without him, and I look forward to us growing old together.

Speaking of growing old, I had another birthday this past week. Actually, it was Thursday. April First…Yes, April Fools, and for the life of me I can't see the humor in that…so STOP LAUGHING!

Of course, for those people who know me at all, they seem to think all of that makes perfect sense. I guess the more I think about it, perhaps it does. The good thing about having such a famous birth date is that once somebody knows, they never seem to forget.

Times being as they are, the gift giving was a little slim this year, however. I was expecting my minions of readers to send money since packages cost so much to ship, but I guess times are just hard. It's the thought that counts, I suppose.

And this was just no ordinary birthday. This one was the big

FIVE-O...that's right. 50. I am having a hard time thinking of myself as getting older.

Yes, it is true that I cannot do a lot of the things I used to. My back stiffens a little more quickly while doing the yard work, and what little hair I have left on my bald little head is beginning to gray a bit.

I usually grow a beard over the winter months, and it is just about entirely gray. In the past year or so, I figure I have earned every one of those gray hairs.

But I have to tell you that the best present I got for this birthday came from a little lady whom I had just met for the first time. She said, "You need to have them change your picture in the newspaper".

"Why is that?" I inquired

"You have lost a lot of weight, and that picture makes you look fat."

"Well, I appreciate your honesty, but I think I will just leave that old fat picture for everyone to see. After all, it makes me feel better when folks like you tell me I've lost weight."

You just can't package a better birthday gift than that.

My Own Little Sack of Rocks to Tote Around

WE ALL HAVE MEMORIES OF THE stories our parents told us growing up that were meant to encourage us to accept the mundane tasks of life or to inspire us to do more than we thought we were capable of doing or to communicate that no matter how badly we saw our plight, our parents always had it worse. In a lot of ways, I guess I even used those stories to make the same point with my own children.

For instance, everyone remembers the old "walk to school in six feet of snow, uphill both ways" story. I can't remember how old I was before that logic fell apart, but I do think, in the beginning at least, I was a little in awe of what my parents had to endure in order to make better chances for me.

Hold onto that thought. I'll come back to it.

I worry about how tough the kids of today are. I know we live in economic times that are rough on some families, but the days of watching young people struggle through adversity in order to improve their station seems to be a bygone era.

But that is a story for another day.

My wife and I have decided that we would use our free time this summer to do a little yard improvement work. You see, she has been watching far too many of those Saturday morning home and yard improvement shows. Consequently, she has a lot of new ideas she has been trying out around the house.

Our latest endeavor is to replace all of the straw beds around our house with rock. Now on the surface, that sounded like a good idea to me. After all, rock doesn't have to be replaced every year. Our kids aren't around anymore to throw them into one another, and other than the fact that Otis, our chocolate lab, eats one occasionally, the whole rock thing sounded pretty good.

So off to the rock store we went, which is another thing that bothers me a little bit. When I was a kid growing up in the heart of pine tree country, who would have ever imagined that one could make a living selling the pine staple that once blanketed my boyhood yard? In fact, we used to rake the stuff into piles and burn it, one of the finer experiences in every boy's pyrotechnic training.

Same for rocks. Who ever hear of buying rocks?

But buy rocks we did, and for two days last week we built a rock pathway down by our flag pole and started putting egg rock in our flower beds. Just so you know, the old boys down at the rock store sell rock by the ton. For those of you a little rusty on your conversion chart, one ton equals two thousand pounds.

I bought two tons of egg rock which even by my rusty math standards equals four thousand pounds. Of course, I could have paid extra to have the rock boys deliver my new bed cover, but instead I drove out to the rock yard, had them dump a ton onto my little trailer, and headed back home to diligently disperse my rocks.

I have a little red wagon I hook to the back of my trusty John Deere lawn tractor, and for two days I dutifully shoveled egg rock from the back of my equipment trailer to the little red wagon and then again shoveled it from the little red wagon into the respective flower bed.

It was at some point in between three and four thousand pounds, while sweating profusely, my lower back aching from the eight-hour experience, that it hit me.

One of the stories my dad used to tell me to demonstrate the importance of commitment and perseverance was that any job worth doing was worth doing well. He used the example of moving a pile of dirt from one place to another to show that no matter how stupid that sounded, if one were to be given that task, then it should be attacked with perfect vigor and attention to detail.

In fact, I think he even had me move several dirt piles from one place to another during my formative years just to solidify the point.

He kept telling me the old "move the pile of dirt" lesson would come in handy one day.

As I dutifully moved my pile of rocks from one place to another, one shovel full at a time, I finally got the point of all of that training he subjected me to long ago.

So there you have it. All of those stories our parents told us that we all thought were hogwash really are beneficial. Thanks, Dad. My back will never be the same.

Rolling in the Grass With my Dog

MY DOG, OTIS, AND I WERE in the yard recently. I was doing yard work, and he was just enjoying being a dog.

One minute he was right up under my feet; the next he was chasing butterflies; the next he was begging to be scratched behind the ears. That last thing makes him more like his master than I care to admit, although I prefer a good back-scratching to being scratched behind the ears.

I swear this dog of mine is about half human, and as far as I can tell, he has two speeds. Stop and wide open. Hold onto that thought. I'll come back to it.

Of course every dog owner thinks his or her dog is one of the family. Take my son and his wife, for example. Now I could tell you this story by just getting directly to the point to say that they got a dog, rescued it from the pound, nursed it back to health, and everybody lived happily ever after.

But somehow I get the idea that you know me better than that.

Remember now that Son Number One is a scientist. A chemist, to be exact. My favorite daughter-in-law is a social scientist, so you can only imagine how the selection process went for this puppy.

Mr. Analytical mind collected all of the information, shopped around, studied breeds, and made every attempt to make the dog selection process as much of a scientific one as is possible. His wife, on the other hand, just wanted a dog to love. That's what social scientists do.

So they settled on a mangy little critter they named Charlie.

Of course he is cute as a button, and I think it is funny to listen to everyone speculate on his breed. He looks like a mutt to me, but regardless of the dispute over his pedigree, we all agree that he is adorable. After all, what's not to love right?

So the entire bunch comes to my house for Thanksgiving. Now just so you know, my dog is named Otis...after the town drunk on Andy Griffith...which is another story altogether...and if he were a child... which technically he is since he just turned two years old, and as I understand the doggie year thing, that makes him about fourteen...an age, by the way, that coincides with the age at about which I threatened to disown my blood offspring...but I digress...

If my dog were a human, I figure he would be at least six-foot-five and weigh about 310 pounds...all muscle I might add...and would have probably been courted by every Division I school in the nation...even at fourteen! Instead, he is just a dog...a very big dog, and he loves more than anything to play with people as if they were dogs.

So when Charlie the granddog...has a nice little ring to it, don't you think?... came for Thanksgiving, I turned Otis...The Beast, as he is affectionately known around here...loose on this newest family member...by the way, Charlie is about half the size of Otis on his best day.

What ensued was forty-eight hours of rough and tumble, ball chasing, mouth slobbering playtime that just about ran us and the dogs ragged. Footnote: Somebody should write a book about dog slobber... makes me grin just thinking about it...gotta be akin to Silly Putty for all of the potential uses...note to self: Next book idea...dog slobber... again, I digress...

I do love my dog. After all, we also refer to him around here as the cancer dog, as his arrival at my house coincided with the news that I had cancer. I give him great credit for being my sounding board for things I needed to say that I just couldn't burden anybody else with...I know; don't end a sentence with a preposition, but this is The South.

Now Otis is an outside dog. He lives well, but number one, he is too big to live indoors, and number two, my mama would roll over in her grave if she knew I let a dog live in the house. Charlie is an inside dog, and when I went down for a recent visit...our first as grandfather and granddog…he slept right at the foot of the bed with me and his grandmother.

I think that is every boy's dream…to have a dog curl up at the foot of the bed while he sleeps. My wife said a stuffed animal was about a close as I was going to get…to a dog to sleep with, I mean…which is not to say that sleeping with my wife is parallel to anything akin to sleeping with a dog…there goes that digress thing again…

But lately I have been letting Otis come inside and sit with me while I work. He has his own little bed right next to my desk, and it has taken me about a month, but he instantly responds to the command "bed up" where he curls up on his pallet and sadly looks at me as if to say, "I'd rather be rolling in the grass, but if this is as close as I get to companionship, then I'll take it."

By the way, I just gave Otis a bath…his first one in about three months…remember he is an outside dog…a very, very big outside dog…and it wore him out so badly that he is lying on his bed sound asleep as I bang away at the keys on my trusty laptop. Who says you can't teach an old dog new tricks?

Oh, one other thing: One of these days I am going to try rolling around in the grass just like Otis. Just my way of staying connected to Man's Best Friend. Here's to hoping you find a reason to roll around in the grass, too.

That Lake Heron Seems Familiar

BY THE TIME YOU READ THIS column, the second anniversary marking my mother's losing battle with cancer will have come and gone. It's hard to think about someone's death as an anniversary because in most cases we associate death and dying with bad things and anniversaries with good things.

Be that as it may, I know there are days when everyone of us in the family misses her – which is bad. The fact that she no longer suffers – and she suffered through the disease a long time – is good.

But this column isn't really about the sad memories of loved ones lost. It is more about how we celebrate those memories through some funny or satisfying reminder we have about the people in our lives that moved us but are no longer around to see the benefits of their labor.

My mother loved the lake perhaps as much as I do. She was never really a big fan of the water so much as she just loved to sit in the swing and take in all of the lake life that goes on right before one's very eyes.

Geese flying down the run of the river and screeching to a halt as they bump their little bottoms along the water's surface…little duck families that emerge in the spring and spend the summer growing up around you…and herons…Yes, the herons.

My mother loved the herons. I don't know if we have blue herons or grey herons or white herons around these parts. Perhaps you really smart Audubon types can enlighten me as to the exact species. No matter, really; she just loved them.

In a lot of ways, I think she identified with their spirit. The sleek birds monitor the shoreline around my house as if they are in charge of something although nobody knows exactly what. They are tall and large, relative to other forms of lake life, and they stand out along the banks of the river if you know how to look for them.

They are just as likely however, to blend in perfectly with their surroundings in such a ways as to go undetected even by the most acute observer. Generally, they are quiet birds until they have something to say, and then they squawk loudly enough to be heard within a three county radius.

If you are quiet and unpretentious, you can get pretty close to a heron. They do, however, have some predetermined space around them within which they do not allow intrusion. When this space is violated, they fly away quickly, squawking that familiar cry just for good measure.

My mama used to say that when she died she was coming back as a lake heron, and the more I think about it, the characteristics of the herons that live around my house suited her just fine.

Just for the record, I don't have any idea if people who die can actually come back as anything. For vocabulary purposes, that is the definition of reincarnation. I know some people believe in that, but the truth of the matter is, for me at least, it really doesn't matter. For purposes of this story, however, it is something to at least consider. After all, if God could send his Son in the form of a human to live among mankind, then surely he could choose to let my mama come back as a heron just to check on things.

Case in point.

One day last week, Otis and I had been for our morning jog. Otis is my chocolate lab, and he looks forward to our morning jaunts about as much as I do. For the record, Otis is not a heron fan. In fact, one of his favorite pastimes is to chase them away from our yard when they come for a visit.

As we walked up the drive onto our carport that has a really cool view of the water, stately standing on the runway of our dock just as pretty as you please was a heron. And in just as coincidental a fashion as that, I had the distinct feeling that it was her.

I know. It all seems a little hokey, but Otis was the first one to spy her...I mean the heron. He looked over his shoulder at me as if to say,

"Not me, Brother. I've heard all those stories you guys tell about how fierce she can be. I'm not running her off!"

And for what seemed like an hour but in reality was only a few minutes, I sat in one of those high back chairs on the deck under the carport, propped my feet up on the rail, and just watched. Without much fanfare at all and as if it were as natural as a weekend visit, I began to have this conversation in my head with my mother.

As I was talking, she...I mean the heron...walked along the sea wall as if to survey everything I had done with the place since the last time she'd seen it. Not particularly in a hurry, she...I mean the heron... craned her neck as if to give me an approving glance.

And in what seemed like the same instant, I said the last word in my head, and she...I mean the heron...flew away. Quietly, this time, as if there really wasn't anything further to say.

I sat for a long time in that chair with Otis lying at my feet. Mr. Hyperactivity almost never takes a break, but I could tell by the look on his little face that he got it, too.

The fact of the matter is that there probably isn't much truth to the notion that upon passing people come back to earth as animals. But every time I see a heron on the lake, I get a little happy inside on the outside chance that my mama might just be checking up on me.

The Man Cave and my Best Friend

Okay. I know this has already been done, but I just can't help the fact that I feel compelled to introduce you to my puppy, and I use that term loosely. His name is Otis.

We named him after the character on Andy Griffith. I will let you draw your own conclusion as to how that came about.

There are a couple of points worth mentioning. When I say this has already been done, I mean that in two ways. Way number one is that there was an entire book written about a crazy dog named Marley. In fact, they even turned it into a full length motion picture.

Way number two is that about six months ago, I wrote my first column about my wayward little pup. At the time, he was about ten pounds of brown fur, and just looked like he might grow up into something that resembled a grizzly bear.

Today, he weighs upward of sixty pounds, and I'll swear he makes Gentle Ben look like a field mouse.

In fact, the more that I think about it, I am not sure at all that he is not part horse. I say that, because my good friend, Robin White, also raises horses. She is responsible for bringing Otis into our lives, and I am certain she wanted me to believe that he is all dog.

Now that I have seen the size of this monster, I am also certain she found some way to breed horses with chocolate labs. Thus, the little bundle of chocolate fur that I brought home six months ago now more closely resembles one of the horses I saw roaming her pasture when Mama and I went to collect little Otis to relocate him to his new home.

I mentioned last week that I have been busy building a workshop in my backyard. Every man should be so lucky, and my wife has been lovingly referring to my new space as the "Man Cave".

I do not contest that nomenclature. In fact, I acknowledge that if a man cave is where a man and his best friend escape to contemplate the wonders of the world, then I do, in fact, have one.

Since I got the heat hooked up, Otis and I retreat to my little man cave, and I spend about two hours each week coming up with the creative genius of which you have become accustomed.

I mention the heat, because that is a man cave dream. If you have ever had one of those back yard shops, then you know that the winter months are difficult. Often cold and rainy, winter days end much too early, and us man cave types are relegated to doing our heavy thinking in the house.

But on this particular night, man's best friend and I are settling in to write my weekly column.

Now my shop is still a little cluttered with pieces of scrap wood, and this just turns into a veritable playground for Otis. I have decided that he has a digestive system of steel. I have never known a dog that could eat two-by-fours like Puppy Chow.

Of course, I recently discovered the orange earplugs went missing that I use when I run my backpack blower. I also noticed that when Otis pooped some days later, his bodily function had an odd color to it. Upon closer investigation, I solved the mystery of the missing earplugs.

I guess framing lumber doesn't stand a chance if earplugs aren't sacred!

It didn't take my puppy turned farm animal long to outgrow the very first little bed we bought him. My wife, bless her heart, bought our little holy terror a new "big boy" bed. Just like his human counterpart, my little buddy just couldn't pass up the chance to taste his new sleeping quarters.

It took about three days, but he tore up all of the little green, fuzz-like stuffing from its insides and summarily ate most of it. How do I know that he ate it? Refer to the lines three paragraphs above except this time the color was green.

In case I forgot to mention it, my little buddy is an outside dog. Don't feel too sorry for him, though. After all, this is a dog that is hardwired to swim in forty-degree water.

Not only that, but our morning routine consists of me taking two doggie treats out to his pen where I let him out, take him to the adjacent wooded area, and engage in baby talk until he both pees and poops. One treat after he pees; one treat after he poops.

Come to think of it, most of his life revolves around peeing and pooping. Unless of course you consider his eating habits. Hold that thought. I'll come back to it.

Following the treat routine, we come inside the house, find Mama in the bedroom, and she baby talks him for a while and rubs behind his ears. He likes that. So do I. Like father, like son.

Now that he is part moose, he can jump up on the bed from a standing position, which he does immediately following the entire rubbing behind the ears routine. He then watches the weather and sports on television before heading back to the living room where we rough house on the steps leading to the upstairs bed room.

He then drinks voraciously out of the toilet in the hall bathroom, and that usually takes us right up to so hungry he is about to pass out.

Meal time is another adventure altogether. You would think a dog that eats like a goat would seldom be hungry. Not so.

Six cups of food every day! Three in the morning, and three in the afternoon. And that doesn't count the whole doggie treat routine. Oh, did I mention that he also eats twigs, pine cones, and leafy shrubs? Just the other day, I watched him eat a pine sapling in three bites!

But in spite of his affinity for eating anything that does not eat him first, he is my love. He is always happy, he never talks back, and he has the memory of a nanosecond. He is clumsy and goofy and spastic…and really, really funny.

And no matter how tired I am or how stressful the day has been, he makes me want to play. And that makes me happy.

HOLiDays

A Mother's Day to Remember

I RECENTLY HAD THE HONOR OF attending two Relay for Life events in the same evening. I reside in Putnam County, and I took part in the survivor's walk at the Putnam County Relay for Life. In case you missed it, I am a survivor of prostate cancer.

Of course, I am a little embarrassed about how easy my treatments went when I hear stories about those who have overcome extraordinary experiences for long periods of time. They are truly survivors and my heroes.

For example, I recently hooked up with an old high school friend of mine on Facebook who had just overcome brain cancer. She experienced a surgery, a large number of radiation treatments, and a year of chemotherapy. She has now been in remission for five months.

Now, that is a survivor!

On the same day I walked my first survivor lap, I also served as the speaker for the luminary program at the Relay for Life in a neighboring county. I'm really not sure why they asked me, but I appreciate the opportunity.

The Luminary program is special. In case you are unfamiliar with the tradition, a bag is filled with sand and a candle is situated in the sand, lit, and burns in honor or memory of someone who has fought in the battle against cancer.

The combination of the soft candle light dancing against the night's darkness, and the respectful silence that accompanies the moment is magical. It's hard to explain if you've never experienced it, but it is the kind of magic that everyone ought to experience.

The end of the ceremony was capped off by a walk around the track behind a professional bagpiper who played expertly. Call me old fashioned, but I just love the special brand of music produced by the bagpipe.

Of course, I made it about ten paces when the emotion overwhelmed me, and I started to cry. I don't think the tears had anything to do with my own experience. Instead they had more to do with the fact that it was at that moment that I made the connection between the fact that God has seen fit to allow me to live beyond the disease and my mother did not.

My mother died of lung cancer almost a year ago after a number of years of courageously fighting what proved to be a dastardly disease. I know that the years she enjoyed beyond the diagnosis had much to do with the research ultimately made possible by funds raised and dispersed through the American Cancer Society.

As I reflect on all of the individuals in the Middle Georgia area who contribute to the tens of thousands of dollars raised annually to continue the fight against cancer, I am overcome with a debt of gratitude for the contribution that research has made to my own hope for a complete cancer cure.

Tomorrow is Mother's Day, and this will be the first Mother's Day we will experience without my mother. I wish she could be here because so much is going on in my family that I know she would have enjoyed.

In a little over a moth, my oldest son will get married, my little boy will turn twenty-one in a week, and she would have enjoyed celebrating my victory over cancer. Spring was her favorite time of year, and she loved the various expressions of flowers that dot the colorful landscape around our yard.

Down by the lake, we had an amazing outburst of yellow from daffodils my mother planted many, many years ago. Trudy and I noticed today that we have one yellow and one lavender iris sporting their splendor in the first flower bed ever planted in our yard. My mother planted those, too.

Yellow and purple were her favorite colors, and they have become sort of the adopted coat of arms around my yard. I don't think we meant to do it intentionally, but those wonderful colors remind us of the contribution my mother made to a strong and prosperous family.

While for me this Mother's Day is bitter sweet, the sweet firmly outweighs the bitter. If you are fortunate enough to see or talk to your mother today, I encourage you to wish her happiness. If something separates you from her, I pray that you will find the courage to bridge that divide – whether it is deserved or not.

And if your mother enjoyed flowers like mine did, then I hope you will find the time to send her a few. If you need ideas for colors, well, yellow and purple are my personal favorites.

A Father's Day gift that Money won't Buy

TOMORROW IS FATHERS' DAY, AND FRANKLY up until now I hadn't really given it much thought. I did call my dad and arrange for me and my wife to take him to dinner later today, but with both of my children out of town and unable to get home, the whole Fathers' Day thing just hadn't really registered with me much.

Hold that thought. I'll come back to it.

In the meantime, here is a story that may not mean very much to most of you, but given my recent luck with trips to Atlanta, I figure it is worth telling.

You may remember from last week that I spent the night in the airport in Atlanta about three weeks ago. To make a long story short, and in case you missed it, Brian, my Navy boy, was trying to get his girlfriend, Morgan, to Chicago for a Memorial Day visit. There was a terrible thunderstorm about the time the plane was scheduled to take off... which, by the way, was 7:30 PM. That will become significant later... which eventually led to the cancellation of the flight entirely, my second trip to the airport in less than twelve hours, standing in line for half of those, and a fitful night's sleep on the floor at old Atlanta-Hartsfield-Jackson International Airport...or whatever they call it now.

I have a few other names for it, but none of them are suitable for reprint in such an upstanding publication as this one.

I think it was over breakfast after our night of sleeping on the floor that I told Morgan while she was currently experiencing the trip from hell, eventually it would just be one of those funny stories we tell over Thanksgiving dinner. I'm not there yet, mind you, but I am beginning to smile a little inside over the entire ordeal.

Early this past week, I was telling my good friend and sometimes golf partner, Jimmy Dillard, that I had pre-purchased a bunch of tickets to Braves games and that we should go sometime. You may be asking what that little piece of information has to do with my recent airport experience. Be patient: I'm getting there.

Just in case you were wondering, I remind you that Jimmy is my sometimes golf partner because an outing in which we participated a few years back resulted in a column I wrote about the Mike and Jimmy rules of golf. Jimmy got a lot of mileage out of that column as it resulted in many of his friends wanting to see the entire Mike and Jimmy Golf Rules Book.

He was assured that it would be an instant best seller if we could just get it into publication because all of his friends would buy at least one. Obviously, Jimmy has more friends than I do.

Be that as it may, I am no closer to writing that book than I am to closing the deal on any other. Consequently, the Library of congress and the New York Times Best Seller list are safe.

Now Jimmy loves baseball. In fact, from what I understand, he was quite a player in his younger days. After some minor arm twisting, we agreed that we would take off Wednesday evening after he got off from work to catch the Braves and the Mets at Turner Field.

Which is exactly what we did.

As a matter of reference, the first pitch of the ballgame was scheduled for 7:10. Atlanta traffic wasn't bad at all, and I have mastered the art of finding an easy parking place at the stadium. Consequently we were in our seats well in advance of the scheduled start time.

The field crew had put the finishing touches on the infield, the PA announcer had covered the starting line ups, and I had my trusty bag of roasted peanuts and favorite adult beverage when I noticed a dark cloud beginning to form over the northwestern rim of the stadium.

Before I could say anything, the wind picked up a bit, mitigating the 90 degree heat, and the field crew scrambled for the tarp that covers the infield during heavy rains. Not a good sign.

Jimmy and I looked at each other with just a slight degree of uncertainty, but before he could ask, I told him I was committed to staying until the final pitch…no matter what. I know how much Jimmy hates to leave a game early.

Let me get to the point. Sometime around 7:30 PM, the skies opened up, torrential rain fell, and marble sized hail rained down from heaven long enough to make the green grass of the outfield look like it had a bad case of dandruff.

My wife, who I neglected to say accompanied us on this trip…after all, guys that make up their own rules of golf obviously need responsible, adult supervision…looked at me with an accusing eye and pointed out that this Atlanta trip was turning out exactly like the last one – minus the cancelled airplane flight…to which she quickly surmised that I represented the common link between disaster and trips to Atlanta.

I don't know how these things always turn out to be my fault, but if you are a guy and have been married more than a minute, then you know where I am coming from. Just so you know, Mama and I are supposed to be taking our own little Chicago trip with Morgan in about two weeks.

So I got informed at the ballgame that I had to drive while she and Morgan fly. I'm still trying to deal with the logic of that, but I remind you I've been married more than a minute.

Oh, just a footnote about taking my wife to the game. Did I mention that during this little thunderstorm the air temperature dropped 30 degrees? Of course we came dressed for the 90 degree version, and midway during the second rain delay as Trudy stood shivering on the concourse, Jimmy threw in the towel, and we left the game early.

Thanks, Baby.

So, what does all of this have to do with Fathers' Day?

My Navy son sent me a short e-mail a few days ago that, among other things, had two declarative statements in it. He is working through a few issues in his life that are just part of growing up, and he had called me earlier to try to talk through some of his thoughts and ideas.

Now he is 22 years old, and every bit his own man. But we had one of those father-son chats that turned out just like you might script it on The Andy Griffith Show.

And his e-mail? Well, it said two things: "Thanks", and "I love you."

Money just won't buy a Fathers' Day gift like that.

From Thanksgiving to Christmas – With Love

WELL, THANKSGIVING HAS COME AND GONE, and I have to tell you that after a week of being back in my normal routine, I am just about worn out. I could get used to this not having to work thing. Some people say they would go crazy in retirement. I just don't see how.

It is funny how at about two-o'clock every afternoon this week, I got sleepy. Maybe it had something to do with the fact that two o'clock coincides with my hammock time over the holidays.

Who'd-a-thunk it? I guess life has to get back to normal sooner or later.

Am I the only one who has noticed or did the Christmas season begin just before Thanksgiving? It seems that every year the commercialization of the holiday season begins earlier and earlier. I figure it won't be long before we skip Thanksgiving entirely. After all, we eat turkey and dressing at Christmas, too. Why not just skip the entire Thanksgiving thing and move right into Ho, Ho, Ho!?

As badly as I hate to admit it, my wife has fallen prey to the same confused Christmas with Thanksgiving mentality. When we were much younger and our kids were little, we absolutely refused to put up a tree prior to about the second week in December.

Now, we go out the day after Thanksgiving, buy the tree, and hang it immediately.

I have been studying the reason for this phenomenon, and I have concluded that the fact that we have fallen for the accelerated Christmas season has to do with the fact that our kids are grown, and we pretty much have an empty nest.

Think about it. When our kids were little, about two weeks of

Christmas hype was all we could stand. Consequently, we put off the tree and decorating and visiting Santa at the mall as long as we could.

I think we miss all of that now, and so we dive right into the Christmas spirit. At first, I resisted, but when Mama says we are getting a tree, well suffice it to say that my only role in the matter is to make sure it gets from the back of the truck to its appointed place in the house.

Don't let me mislead you. I love Christmas and the season of tinsel, giving, and caroling as much as anyone. And the truth of the matter is that I have kind of gotten a little caught up in the early sounds of Christmas myself.

Case in point. I have *A Statler Brothers Christmas* downloaded to my Ipod, and while I was listening to the random playing of tunes recently, the Statler version of Away in a Manger began playing. I just love the four part harmony of arguably one of the greatest musical talents of all time.

I listened to the other various Christmas selections on my way to work, and as I walked into the office I found myself whistling Christmas carols of various styles and sorts. Christmas carols make me feel good.

And then it hit me. I think we rush to jump into Christmas because the entire season makes us feel good. For the time that we focus on buying gifts for those special individuals in our lives, for every instance that we greet someone we know and even those whom we don't with "Merry Christmas", and for every rendition of White Christmas we listen to on the radio, Christmas just makes us feel good.

The more I think about it, Thanksgiving begins the season of love, and Christmas just makes it a little longer. And, if there is one thing this world can use more of, it is love.

You Can't Make This Stuff Up

It was exactly one year ago that I began my weekly column for the Union Recorder. The past year has been a lot of fun, and I hope you have enjoyed getting to know me, my family, my work, and all of the goofy ideas I have about life and how it ought to be lived.

I looked back at that first column, and since it coincided with the Thanksgiving season, you guessed it. I wrote about those things for which I was thankful.

I thought about the whole thankfulness thing again this year as I began rolling ideas around in my head for my obligatory Wednesday night creativity session, but I figured every columnist worth his or her salt had already done it.

But, it is, after all, Thanksgiving, and so rather than bore you with the usual sappy thankfulness speech, I decided to give you a mental picture of Thanksgiving from the Rowland perspective. So, here goes.

The tradition in my family for years was to gather at my house for the Thanksgiving feast. Of course, that was when my entire family lived in the same town or in relative close proximity.

My wife and I were the first to have children, so we were also the first to be able to stand behind the declaration that our children needed to receive the meal of all meals at home. My sister's children came much later, and it was only when I moved away from home that the rest of my family caught on to the stay at home ruse.

I was going to try it again this year, but my sister lives 2000 miles away, and both sets of parents are beginning to experience the kind of health issues that make it next to impossible to travel very far from home.

I tell you all of that to say this: Trudy and I left the friendly confines of Lake Sinclair early this morning with the sun shining brightly as it rose over the steam kissed lake. My yard was littered with the spectacular fall colors of stubborn leaves trying to hold onto their tree home for just one more week.

The red, yellow, and orange carpet of leaves was a post card picture of the reason, as if I needed one, that we should have stuck to our guns and enjoyed Thanksgiving at home. Not to be, however, and thus began our Thanksgiving journey.

Before I go any further, let me say that I love my family…all of them. In-laws included. But, Jeff Foxworthy's best redneck routine can't hold a candle to the natural comedy that unfolds each time we get together.

I won't tell you where they live, but suffice it to say that they live in a town so small you can look both ways and see all of the traffic lights. I also will not divulge names, because after all, it is important to protect the innocent, something I learned form Dragnet and Adam-12.

Suffice it to say that we had been at my in-laws house about 30 minutes when my oldest son and I decided to walk to the grocery store to pick up a few things that my wife needed for the aforementioned Thanksgiving meal.

Since I live thirty minutes away from anything, walking to the grocery store is a cool thing. Of course we stopped by the hardware store on the way because that is just what guys do when faced with that option.

On the way back to the house, we passed a barber shop where the following sign was prominently displayed in the window facing the road: "No dogs allowed except for those belonging to blind people."

I swear, I could not make this stuff up. My sophisticated college chemistry major of a son just could not help himself. He went over with his camera phone and took a picture for posterity.

If you do not believe me, just catch him around campus this week and ask to see his "blind people dog" picture.

One of the things I appreciate about my in-laws is their simple existence. Going to their home is like a walk back into a time long past. No one gets in a hurry, so after our walk to the grocery store, my son, father-in-law, and I sat on the back porch cracking and eating pecans.

My father-in-law spent the next half hour or so telling us about all of his plans for little construction projects that will most likely go undone for another year. After all, we had this conversation last year, and most of the chore list is the same.

Around dark, we left that sleepy little town for my parent's house, and what I know will prove to be a much faster pace. The hour or so ride home gave me time to reflect, and I have to admit that I did not get very much done that day, but I did just take some time off.

I took a nap on the couch, watched some pretty meaningless television, and just sat outside on a perfect South Georgia day. I laughed a little inside about the simple nature of old people who grew up with little sophistication.

It is hard to imagine grown people who cancelled their Internet service because it was too hard to understand or who still cannot use a cell phone effectively.

And, while I really didn't start out to think too deeply about what makes me thankful this season, at least for this Thanksgiving, I am most thankful for the people in my life who remind me to slow down, rest, and be simple.

Those Things for Which I am Thankful

THIS THANKSGIVING MARKS THE THIRD YEAR I have been writing a column for the Union Recorder. I did some rough figuring, and only having missed a handful of weeks for various and sundry reasons, I figure I have written about one-hundred-and-fifty columns.

Now, I am not at all sure when I realized that I had a gift for story telling through the written word, but I am thankful for the talent God has given me and the opportunity He has provided me to share with others. My life is pretty simple and fairly mundane. But, I figure most everyone else has the same simple and mundane existence, and the fact that we find some commonality in that fact means there is hope for the human race.

I am thankful for the talent I have to share the kinds of experiences that are common to all of us. My suspicion is that we are all more alike than we are different. If over the past three years, my writing has touched you in some way, then I am thankful for that, too.

This will be the first Thanksgiving without my mother. She died back in July after a long battle with cancer. I am thankful she isn't suffering anymore, but I think today, more than any other time, I missed her.

There is a song by Diamond Rio entitled *I Believe* that talks about how death cannot separate us if we believe that we are connected to one another beyond this world by forces that are more powerful than human understanding…that there are times when the presence of someone we love deeply can be felt even when they are absent….

I was listening to this song on the way to work last week, and all of the emotion of missing my mother kind of caught me off guard. Before I realized what was happening, a steady stream of tears began to trace the outline of my cheeks, and I realized how thankful I am for what she meant to our family. In some strange way, we all carry some piece of her constitution, and I am convinced we are better people because of it.

Oh, I am thankful for music, too. Sometimes music touches us in ways that prose never can. I wish I could sing, but I really can't carry a tune in a bucket. I figure, however, that as long as I am in my truck by myself, then who can hear. Right?

If you see me riding down the road with my head thrown back like a howling dog in the moonlight, then you will know that I am living out my fantasy of being a country music star. Trust me. It is only a fantasy.

Trudy and I recently became parents again. That's right. Parents. I know what you are thinking. At our age we should know better. Right?

The truth of the matter is that we are parents to a little brown ball of fur with four legs and sharp little canine incisors that can cut through even the toughest leather glove. It's funny how a simple little puppy can bring so much joy to one's life.

One night last week, my new little buddy and I sat together by a warm fire out in my back yard. I talked to him about stuff in general. He never said a word, never complained, and only grunted occasionally as I rubbed behind his little ears. A friend like that is hard to find.

Tom T. Hall once sang a song about old dogs, children, and watermelon wine. Old dogs begin as puppies, and I am looking forward to watching my little guy grow old with me. I have a theory that the reason men generally stink at relationships is because most of us experienced the unconditional love of a good dog early in our lives.

With the love of a good dog serving as the standard against which all relationships are judged, we really never stood a chance.

Speaking of children, this will be the first Thanksgiving since they were born that both of my kids won't be home for the annual family gathering. Life is changing, and I am not sure how I feel about that. Seeing them grow into responsible young adults who can function without parental support is every parents dream, and I am no different. I am very proud of what they have been able to accomplish.

This will also be the first Thanksgiving that Son Number One has a fiancé. I am thankful for her and what she means to him. Perhaps more importantly, I am thankful for what she brings to our family. We are all lucky to have her in our future.

Son Number Two now has a part-time job, and I am very thankful for that. Anything to get them closer to someone else's payroll. He is also good looking, handsome, and responsible. He doesn't cause me any trouble or embarrassment, and I am thankful for that, too.

My little boy is twenty-years old and at the end of every conversation, be it over the telephone or in person, he always says, "I love you, Dad." I am most thankful for that.

I am thankful for early detection of prostate cancer. I have it, and I am still not sure how I feel about that, either. It all sounds more ominous than I think it really is, but I still wish I didn't have it.

I am, however, now a believer in regular screenings for men after age forty. It really is painless and it can be the difference between life and death. Modern medicine is an amazing thing. Who would have ever believed that cancer of any kind can be cured? In a way, that in and of itself is a miracle...I am thankful for miracles, too.

I worry about the world in general. People still hate one another because of the color of their skin or the place where they grew up. Wars used to be fought over territorial conquest. In a way, that makes sense to me. You want more land, you fight another country for it. Whoever wins gets the land.

Today, we fight because we hate. Hate takes a long time to heal. Perhaps it never does. In spite of that, I still think we live in the greatest nation on Earth. The choices we have to celebrate Thanksgiving and Christmas are evidence of that. Perhaps we are more politically correct than we should be, and perhaps we should stand up for what we believe more often, but I am thankful for the opportunity to live, work, and worship in this great nation. With all of her flaws, she is still worth fighting for.

The truth is, the more I think about all of the things for which we all have to be thankful, I realize there just isn't enough room in this column space to say it all. So next year, I think the newspaper ought to just dispense with all of the bad news for the day, and we all ought to just send them pages and pages and pages of things for which we are all thankful.

For one day, let's just put the inevitable negativity of human nature behind us and fill up the newspaper with positive thoughts. Just think. If we could put more positive things than negative in every local newspaper in the country, then that would really be something for which to be thankful.

Happy Thanksgiving.

Another Year of Things for Which I am Thankful

WELL, IT'S THAT TIME AGAIN. I can't believe another Thanksgiving has come and gone. It's funny how the year I was fifteen years old seem to crawl by. I know it is the same 365 days of any other year, but turning sixteen just seemed to take forever.

At fifty, the years fly by. I wonder why that is? Regardless, I am thankful that God has seen fit to allow me another year on His planet.

Speaking of God, have you noticed the beautiful full moon this past week? At my house, the moon rises to the east. As it clears the tree line, the bright moonlight dances and shimmers off the run of the Oconee River which twists and turns in the same direction.

The moon is pretty in the summer, but there is something about a winter moon that is particularly captivating. I know we haven't had much cold weather lately, but the cold, crisp winter nights are on their way. Standing outside in the cold air, my breath thickening against the winter chill, and experiencing the "daylight" of a full moon is one of those experiences for me that is hard to beat.

As thankful as I am for the moon, I am especially thankful for the God who created it and for his willingness to take the form of a man so that I might experience a close personal relationship with Him. I know some people think the whole relationship with God thing is a little hokey, but my personal relationship with God is what takes seemingly random acts that occur in my world and gives them meaning.

My sister was in charge of the Thanksgiving dinner this year. We trade it off from year to year, not exactly following any schedule, but we always seem to know who gets it next.

The truth of the matter is that Thanksgiving dinners in our family have kind of turned into "open to the public" kinds of events. We don't really have a very large or very close extended family, and we figure if we are going to go to the trouble of cooking the all encompassing Thanksgiving meal with the trimmings then we might as well have a crowd.

Eighteen people later, we enjoyed a meal fit for a king. I am thankful for all of those people, family and otherwise, who enjoyed the once again amazing turkey and dressing.

We have a dog named Otis. Otis is my cancer dog. He came to our house about the time I started treatments for prostate cancer, and he has rapidly stolen the hearts of everyone in the family.

The lady who gave him to me raises horses, and Otis is nearly as big as one. I kid her about crossbreeding a dog with a horse because this mutt is huge.

Otis is an outside dog, and we bring him with us to my sister's house when we come. He loves to travel, and my sister has a dog named Ellen. No one is really sure what breed Ellen is or her exact age. We just know she is old.

Otis is still about half puppy, and he wants desperately to play with Ellen. Ellen is too old for his foolishness, and occasionally growls and snaps at him just to keep him in his place. I think my sister gives Ellen the doggie equivalent of Prozac when she finds out Otis is coming because he just about drives her crazy with his child-like antics.

I am thankful that Ellen is too old to really put Otis in his place. Lord knows she wants to.

All of my children were home again at one time which doesn't happen often enough anymore. I am thankful for that.

Steven and Meghan got married last summer, have a nice little life going in Florida, and are a really cute couple. Meghan is my favorite daughter-in-law. Of course, she is my only daughter-in-law, but we don't squabble over details. She is also my intellectual equal. Actually, she is probably smarter than me, but she is too young to know that so let's just keep that as our little secret.

I am thankful for secrets, too. We just don't have to know everything.

Brian will be leaving for the Navy in a couple of months. I am not yet sure how I feel about that, but I will tell you this. There is no one I would rather having defending me than my youngest son. I sleep better at night knowing that the United States military really does go after the brightest and the best.

This whole Navy thing seems to have provided him with some focus and direction not to mention a paying job, a good place to live, and three square meals a day. I am especially thankful for that.

My father managed to see is 77th birthday this year, is in pretty good shape for his age, and seems to be managing just fine without my mother. She died a couple of years back which makes Thanksgiving a little sad because for all of the years I can remember, this was her day. My mother handled the traditions that now my sister and I carry forward. I know my dad misses her. We all do, but I am thankful for the memories she provided, the traditions that she taught, and the fact that she doesn't suffer anymore.

I was sitting on the front porch at my sister's house Thanksgiving morning, and the wind caused what my wife quite wittingly referred to as raining leaves. I think the changing of the seasons is symbolic of how the seasons of life change. I am not exactly sure what season my life is in right now, but I am contemplating some changes that are ahead of schedule, a little risky, and somewhat out of character for me.

Choices are good, however, and I seem to have a few at this crossroads in my life. I am thankful to have choices.

Speaking of choices, my wife is a saint, a fact that no one in my family will dispute given the fact that we are approaching our 29th anniversary as a team. Of course the sailing hasn't always been smooth, but any choppy seas in our life have always been my doing. Everyone agrees she could have married a doctor or a lawyer, but instead she chose me, the only blemish on what has otherwise proven to be a stellar career in the decision-making department.

I am thankful for the woman who is my best friend, confidant, and head cheerleader. She could have done better, and I have gotten far more than I deserve.

So here's to wishing each of you a happy Thanksgiving Season. May you find time to contemplate all for which you have to be thankful. If that involves people, then don't forget to tell them.

Keeping a Thanksgiving Secret isn't as Easy as it Looks

By the time you read this column, the entire Rowland clan will have pulled off one of the great surprises of all time. The Grandfather of all surprises...hold onto that thought. I'll come back to it.

For the past five years, I have used this space each Thanksgiving to make a list of those things for which I am thankful. My suspicion is that my list isn't much different than many of yours which means that any one of you could have written this column.

Quick footnote: You should try writing to the newspaper sometime. They love getting letters, and it is a real exercise in coherent thinking to write down your thoughts, share them with others, and come to grips with the accountability of the written word.

We live in complicated times. Unemployment is higher than it has been in recent memory, unless of course you are old enough to remember the late 1970's and early '80's when home mortgage interest rates were over 15% and unemployment topped 10%.

While showing signs of recovery, fewer people have good paying jobs or money to spend entering the holiday season and sadly too many people are still losing their homes because they can't pay their mortgage.

In spite of all of that, Americans still enjoy more freedom than any other nation on the planet. Our ability to choose between any number of variables that, in most cases, place each of us in control of our own destiny is second to none.

It is true that our political system is currently undergoing some kind of stress that seems to make us more enemies than friends, but if you studied history in any depth, I think you would find that the political discourse that we now see pales in comparison to that of the early years.

Regardless, there is so much for which to be thankful, and all each of us has to do is take time to seriously inventory our current situation. Even if you face some kind of adversity in your life, the "thankful" list quickly out numbers that "woe is me" list.

So, I am going to dispense with the list thing this year. I encourage each of you to make a list of your own, write it down, and let it become your guide for a positive outlook toward the future.

One of my sons is in the Navy, and he has been away from home since last January. In fact, as far as I know, he hasn't even missed a day of work.

We have been to see him a couple of times, but there is just something about coming home that makes a reunion special. Thus our surprise.

One thing about relationships is that when you fully invest in one, knowing the heart and mind of the other person is easier than you think. My son was looking forward to getting some time off at Christmas and had pretty much resigned himself to the fact that a Thanksgiving appearance was out of the question.

Now just to lend some perspective, Thanksgiving around my house has always been one of those "open to the public" affairs. We may move around from one family member's house to another, but we almost always invite guests who may or may not be exactly family.

Some years we have a house full and others have been more intimate and cozy. But ham, turkey, cornbread dressing, and all of the fixings are a staple.

To make a long story short, I could tell from some of our conversations that what my son needed most was to come home. We talked about it a bit, he figured out he had enough leave to make the trip and still have time off at Christmas, and I agreed to spring for the airline ticket.

Only one other thing: He wanted to keep it a secret from his mother.

Now I have to tell you that I was not entirely supportive of this plan mainly because keeping a secret is not one of my strong suits. And, since I have had to keep this one for about six weeks, it has been doubly tough.

And, since I had to involve all of the family…and I do mean all… in this little deception so that it would make sense to have our annual

Thanksgiving tradition at our house...well, let's just say in keeping with the Navy theme, "Loose lips sink ships."

I have to tell you that the day came off without a hitch. Unless you consider the fact that my wife and I almost got into a fight over the fact that she wanted her parents to Skype with Brian before lunch, and I had to tell her to tend to the dressing and let me handle the technological reunion.

She tried to pop me with the kitchen towel, a slight over reaction I thought.

The best way I know how to describe what ultimately happened is this way:

> Dozens of cell phone calls, text messages, and voice mails: $49.95

> New duffel bag for packing clothes for four day trip home: $35.00

> One roundtrip airline ticket from Great Lakes, Illinois to Eatonton, GA: $369

> The look on Mama's face and the sound of the squeal when, completely to her surprise, her Navy son stepped from around the corner of the house in his dress blue uniform: Priceless.

I tried to say the blessing for the big Thanksgiving meal, and quite frankly, I just couldn't keep it together without crying. There was a lot I meant to say, but the whole crying thing cut my remarks a little short. I'm thankful for a family who understands and appreciates my emotion.

On this one day, however, God absolutely out did himself. As I looked at everyone gathered around the table and what we all mean to each other, it occurred to me that He had exceeded my wildest expectations.

I am thankful for that, too.

The Greatest Story Ever Told

I AM A STORYTELLER. PERHAPS NOT a very good one, but a storyteller just the same. Hang onto that thought. I'll come back to it in a minute.

I recently had the good fortune of attending an out of town meeting in the North Georgia Mountains. As part of the entertainment one evening, my group had the pleasure of listening to bluegrass music performed by a local quartet of musicians.

Now I am a bluegrass music fan. Something about the melodious blend of the guitar, fiddle, mandolin, and banjo create a sound that just seems to define heaven. I know, I know. Legend has it that heavenly music is played with a harp. Don't get me wrong. I like harps. I just think God loves bluegrass music, too.

And the harmony. I am absolutely head over heels in love with the sound of four voices all singing different notes to combine for a sound that will take your breath away. I get chill bumps just thinking about it.

Aside from the music, however, what impressed me most about this little band of two men and two women was the fact that they used their time, talents, and probably money to teach mountain music to school aged children. You know, I think music represents the very soul in a person…the deep down feelings, both happy and sad; it exposes the root of who we are and perhaps even who we hope to become.

No Child Left Behind doesn't measure musical talent. In fact, it doesn't even contemplate that students who are gifted musically have worth equal to those who are gifted in mathematics and English. In case you can't tell, that frustrates me.

Footnote: No Child Left Behind is the federal legislation aimed at holding schools and school systems accountable for gains in student achievement. Likewise, it recognizes the achievement gap between

196

various sub groups and contemplates that schools must do more to close this gap.

None of which, by the way, I disagree with. But not once do the regulations address music or art or drama.

At our little mountain concert, we were engaged with a small group of musicians who had time to talk to us about the work they were doing with students. For example, I found it fascinating that the way mountain families passed down the old ballads for which they are famous was to have adults sit around the porch playing and singing the verses and then requiring the children to recite the verses back to them.

In this way, the musical mountain stories were passed down from one generation to the other. In some way, I am afraid that my generation, and maybe even the next, has lost sight of the importance of stories. We just don't make time for them anymore.

I tell stories because it is the way my mind visualizes almost anything. Stories help me learn. I know facts and figures are important, but the real issue for me is what story do they tell? And what can we learn from the story to improve on the vast, wonderful world that is at our fingertips? More importantly for me, how can we give the stories to our children so that they don't make the same mistakes we did?

I love the Christmas season because it is a time when we celebrate the story of the birth of Jesus. I realize that not everyone views this story with the same relevance with which I do. And frankly, I think that is okay.

The God who created a wonderfully complex mind surely contemplated our need to question the world He created. Regardless, I have included the story of Jesus' birth below for your reading pleasure taken from the Book of Luke, the second chapter, the New American Standard Version.

Now it came about in those days that a decree went out from Caesar Augustus, that a census be taken of all the inhabited earth.

This was the first census taken while Quirinius was governor of Syria.

And all were proceeding to register for the census, everyone to his own city.

And Joseph also went up from Galilee from the city of Nazareth, to Judea, to the city of David, which is called Bethlehem, because he was of the house and family of David in order to register, along with Mary, who was engaged to him, and was with child.

And it came about that while they were there, the days were completed for her to give birth.

And she gave birth to her first-born son; and she wrapped Him in cloths, and laid Him in a manger, because there was no room for them in the inn.

And in the same region there were some shepherds staying out in the fields and keeping watch over their flock by night.

And an angel of the Lord suddenly stood before them, "Do not be afraid; for behold, I bring you good news of a great joy which shall be for all the people; for today in the city of David there has been born for you a Savior, who is Christ the Lord.

And this will be a sign for you; you will find a baby wrapped in cloths, and lying in a manger."

And suddenly there appeared with the angel a multitude of the heavenly host praising God, and saying, "Glory to God in the highest, and on earth peace among men with whom He is pleased."

For me, this is still the greatest story ever told. On this Christmas Day, it is my wish for you that you will find time to spend with family and that during your time together, you will share the stories that link us to our past and define our hope for the future.

If for some reason you find yourself without family during this holiday season, just know that the greatest story ever told is one of hope, love, and peace through grace. May the hope, love, and peace of the holiday season abide with you now and forever.

It's Beginning to Look a lot Like Christmas

WELL, IT'S OFFICIAL. THE ROWLAND HOUSEHOLD is in the Christmas spirit!

Now, I am not exactly sure when it happened, but I can remember a time during my younger years when my wife would chastise with glee the distorted individuals who put up their tree, hung the stockings, and otherwise decorated for Christmas immediately following Thanksgiving. For the last couple of years, however, we have joined the ranks of the trim the tree after Thanksgiving crowd.

Now, in spite of that previous statement, I love the whole tree getting activity. When our boys were little, we would drive to a nearby tree farm, let them select the tree of their choosing, cut it down with a hand saw, drag it back to the truck, and haul it to its eventual pre-Christmas destination.

Now we just go by one of those roadside places where they ship the trees in from somewhere in North Carolina and have them throw it in the back of the truck. Otis, my 98 pound chocolate lab now helps me situate it in the tree stand...which, by the way is a sight to behold... and Trudy has the task of making sure it is true and plumb before it enters its space.

This year, all of that went off without a hitch, which has not always been the case.

So, I started asking myself, "What happened?" How did we fall victim to a tradition that we swore would never infect our Christmas thinking?

I suspect it had something to do with our kids. Even if it didn't, since neither of them is around to defend themselves, why not blame it on them?

As parents, I am sure we knew that once the Christmas spirit was actually let out of the bag, our guys would worry us to death about Santa Clause, what they would get for presents, and when to put up the tree. We also knew that once the tree went up, then it had to have presents underneath, and well, that would just absolutely doom us to begin the Christmas Eve countdown.

Don't get me wrong. There isn't a Scrooge bone in either one of our bodies. But when it comes to children, well we just figured a unified front was the best defense against a Christmas season that would have outlived its welcome even before it started.

Of course thinking about our kids and the Christmas season sent me for a little trip down memory lane. It just seems like yesterday that we were staying up half the night awaiting Santa's arrival so that we could put the few things together that were too large to come down the chimney.

Of course, my children were fortunate. They at least had a chimney. When I was growing up, fireplaces were not the rage, and Ole' Saint Nick had to come through the front door at my house.

I will say this, however; the toys my kids got where a lot cooler than those I received growing up. This is not meant to be a negative slant against my parents. After all, walkie talkies, a Matell M-16 Marauder, and a 10-speed bicycle were hip for my day.

But my kids got things like video games and battery operated trucks. Trudy and I stayed up almost all night one Christmas Eve trying to beat Mario before the kids even got a shot at it.

The battery operated truck, however, was just one of those presents I always envied. This thing was built like a 4-wheel drive monster truck, and even at four or five years old, the boys drove around in that truck as if it were the real thing. I still get a bit jealous just thinking about it.

I tried a couple of times to see if I could actually fit into it out of pure covetousness, but it just wouldn't work. Besides, there was a load limit, the extent to which I far exceeded even in my fit and trim days.

Of course that was a long time ago, and now both of our boys live away from home. We usually talk several times a week, but it just isn't the same as having them ask every time we go to the mall if they can sit on Santa's lap for the umpteenth time…which I think answers my question about how we fell into the trim the tree the day after Thanksgiving trap.

That singular act seems to help jump start the holiday spirit for us both, especially given the fact that there are no little tykes to run around begging for the Christmas spirit to be unleashed.

Ode to Christmas

Twas the night before Christmas and something was askew,
So I thought I would take a minute and share it with you.
Lights were all hung from the streetlamps with care,
While great scenes of commercialism danced through the air.

My wife had bought presents for Kid one and Kid two.
This left her with only Christmas dinner to do.
I, on the other hand, the great planner I am,
Found myself in my usual Christmas Eve jam.

No present for her! No! Not even one.
Well, surely you can see something had to be done.
So, I sprang from the recliner and flew like a flash,
Stepped over the clutter and holiday trash.

My Jeep at the ready, a full tank of gas,
I'd better move quickly lest this feeling not last.
On to Wal-Mart or Penny's or the lingerie store.
Hey, I'll have to think about that last one some more.

Wait! What am I thinking? You're thinking it, too, I'll bet.
Why leave the recliner. Just use the Internet!
So surfing I go through no sea or ocean
That I would be thoughtful just shows my devotion.

To a little old woman so lively and quick...
Oops. Calling her old might not do the trick.

I digress. Now, back to my Internet shopping with glee,
In search of a gift to place under our tree.

I found just the right gift. A thing whatchamadoodle.
And, it works perfectly with last year's noodlescrumfoozle.
That's it! A gift that is said to keep giving,
Long after the thing has ceased to be living.

On second thought I'd better take the Jeep after all
And see what great bargains are left in the mall.
With time running out I'm down to the last minute
I can't go home with a bag and nothing in it.

So I do what any self respecting husband would do
I call up my sister for an idea or two
She is full of ideas and a host of good cheer.
She's also full of other things I won't mention here.

No help was she, so I am back to square one.
This whole last minute shopping thing is really no fun!
On to Sears and Belk and Goody's and such
Santa and his elves haven't helped very much.

When what to my wondering eyes should appear
But an answer to my dilemma and it was always right here
Right under my nose. I'm ashamed of myself.
I hold Santa responsible. You really can't blame the elf.

The answer to my Christmas Eve shopping came late,
And it arrived in the form of a gift certificate
So with a big sigh of relief I head to the house
Once again to be in the good grace of my spouse.

"Next year will be different!" I exclaim with all might,
But for now, Merry Christmas and to all, a good night.

The Christmas Gift That
Keeps on Giving

I JUST LOVE THE CHRISTMAS SEASON. In spite of the way we have commercialized the celebration of the birth of a savior, I do enjoy the act of giving and receiving gifts. I suppose it is only natural to feel that way.

I don't know if you have had this experience, but the gift giving dynamic in the office where I work is interesting to watch. I am fortunate to enjoy those people with whom I work, but Christmas gift giving around the office tells a lot about the culture of those who give the gifts.

Now let me say this before I get into trouble with the people with whom I work. Not everyone gives a gift at Christmas, and that is okay. The truth of the matter is that none of us really need anything, and most of the gifts that get swapped around the office are just your average candy box or cookie tin or the occasional lottery scratch off ticket.

We used to engage in this elaborate scheme over a covered dish luncheon that involved wrapping some kind of gag gift that would be swapped using any number of ingenious methods. The fun of this exercise was more about how creative an individual could be as opposed to the actual gift itself.

Of course that was always a lot of fun, but doing it year after year just meant that the creativity meter went up a little each year making it harder and harder to one up the gift from a previous year. We ditched that tradition a few years ago, and now everyone just kind of does their own thing.

That usually results in the aforementioned box of candy or tin of cookies from those in the office that have the time, inclination, and forethought to pull it off. I, for instance, am not one who gives the office gift giving thing much forethought...if any at all. In fact, I usually just wait around to see if anyone even gives me anything making the assumption that if I get no gift, then there must not be an expectation that the act of giving will be reciprocated in any way.

This year was pretty much like any other year resulting in me getting a couple of candy canes, some party mix, and gingerbread cookies delivered in little Santa pants. That last item pegged the creativity meter for best delivery method.

I kept the cookies and gave the Santa pants to my boss seeing as how my kids are too old to appreciate such frivolity, and my boss has grandchildren who are much more likely to appreciate my sacrifice. I did learn that the Santa pants lady bought them as a prospective Christmas gift some months ago which, by the way, goes along with her work habits of never procrastinating or letting projects fall through the cracks.

You see how this gift thing works? It is kind of like the fact that most dog owners have a dog that either looks a lot like them or that takes on their personality in some fashion.

I, for example, am prone to procrastinate and figure why do today what can be safely, or otherwise, put off until tomorrow. Case in point: I am cramming in this column at the last minute in an effort to meet my deadline with the newspaper.

By the way, you guys down at the newspaper take note. I have been working for the newspaper for awhile now, and I have yet to receive even a Christmas card. No Christmas bonus, no box of candy, no Christmas turkey. Nothing.

You guys know I am only kidding. I am what you might call an "e-employee." Simply stated, I work via e-mail. In fact, I have never set foot in the newsroom...or even the lobby for that matter. Via the wonders of the Internet, I work the virtual highway which I guess really exempts me from the newspaper office gift giving experience if there is one.

I digress. Back to the office shenanigans of my real job which, by the way, the folks down at the paper are quick to point out I should keep.

Thursday I realized that I really hadn't done anything for all of the people in my office. I actually realized it on Wednesday, and I decided to put off doing anything about it for a day to see if my feelings of guilt would go away.

They did not, and on Thursday morning I stopped at Wal-mart, purchased the last 28 remaining little plastic candy canes full of Miniature Reese's Cups, attached a thoughtful "We wish you a Merry Christmas" note, and hand delivered one to all of the girls and boys in my office.

Whew. That was close. Once again I avoided the Scrooge name tag that most assuredly will be affixed to the individual who forgets to at least deliver candy. And just under the wire. Another good deed!

I was actually feeling pretty good about myself until I started looking at the extra candy container I had remaining and started reading the nutrition facts prominently affixed to the container. It was at that moment that I realized that my good deed really wasn't very good at all.

It seems that five pieces of the peanut butter-chocolate candy that has become a household name contains 220 calories. 110 of those calories are from fat. Honestly, I am not sure what that really means, but it can't be good.

The same five pieces contains 5 grams of saturated fat. It seems there are two kinds of fat: trans fat and saturated fat. I really have no idea what the difference is between the two, so I turned to my trusty computer and Googled it.

Let's see…saturated fat seems to be better than trans fat although the information is clear that fat should be avoided. Whew. I thought for a second there I had goofed by giving all of the women in my office a present that would add to their troubles instead of spreading the holiday cheer which was my intention.

Further analysis, however, indicates that there are 25 grams of carbohydrates per serving which translates into about 52 grams per container. I Googled that, too.

It seems that carbs are not all bad. In fact, a normal diet should consist of about 250 grams per day, and these grams should come from….let's see…whole grain bread, cereals and pastas, nuts, seeds, legumes, fruits and vegetables. Nope. No Reese's cups. Oh well…

…and sugars. There are 23 grams of sugars whatever the heck that means. So…you guessed it…I Googled that, too. Let me keep things simple. Sugars are complicated! I am not even going to try to explain what I learned. Suffice it to say that 23 grams of sugars in Reese's Cups is not a good thing.

So now that I have completed my office gift giving experience for the year, I find it necessary to apologize for the gift I gave. Sorry, guys.

Next year you will be getting carrots and celery. Sorry, no ranch dressing. Too many fats, carbs, and sugars.

What Christmas is to Me

I WAS BORN IN 1960, AND I have decided that those who didn't grow up during the '60's and '70's really missed out. Times just seemed simpler then. I know. I know. We had the drug culture, and the hippy movement, flower power, and the anti –establishment era was in full swing.

But for folks like me who were raised by parents with strong conservative values, black and white television, listening to AM radio, and crew cuts are memories to be cherished.

In 1966 I had a crew cut. In 1976, I had shoulder length hair. By 2006, most of my hair had washed down the drain of many a morning shower.

I turned sixteen years old in 1976. My dad gave me a 1966 Volkswagen Beetle, which is a little bit of a misrepresentation of the truth. My memory is that I had five-hundred dollars in the bank. He took two-hundred-fifty of it, and that consummated my first auto purchase.

Looking back on it, the money wasn't a lot, and although it was half of everything I had, I still believe he pretty much gave me the car.

Some thirty-three years later, my kids both drive cars that I bought new, paid for, and gave to them so that they could start their lives as young adults without having to worry about transportation. I have no idea which way is the best, but I imagine that I am like most parents who want to provide more for their children than our parents were able to provide for us.

I hope my kids can do better for their children. In today's world I have my doubts.

My 1966 Beetle had an AM radio, and the only station in my hometown I could receive was a country music station. For some reason, I still remember the call letters: WQCK. So, at a time when most of my friends were listening to heavy metal and rock and roll, I was listening to John Denver, Merle Haggard, and the Statler Brothers.

I really never lost my love for country music, but I must admit that the advent of satellite radio allows me to listen to 70's music full time, and the tunes of my teen-aged years bring back a lot of fond memories.

Of course, I am about as Twenty-First Century as they come. I have an I-pod, and it has on it my favorite songs from the various genres of my upbringing. For those of you who are versed in the I-pod vernacular, one of my playlists is entitled "Christmas Music".

Therein can be found my favorite Christmas music as performed by the Statler Brothers. There is just something magical about the four part harmony of Harold, Phil, Don, and Lew. *Silent Night, Joy to the World, Away in a Manger*…it makes my skin crawl just thinking about it.

Today, of course, we listen to CD's. In my day, we played vinyl LP's (short for long play, meaning a record that played on a turntable for a while). So, I am riding in my truck, lost in the music of yesteryear, and I recognize the familiar sound of one of my favorites: *What Christmas Means to Me.*

Since that time, I have been thinking about what Christmas means to me, and I just wanted to take a minute to share that with you.

I think Christmas is my favorite time of year, because for all of our differences, we all seem to understand that the season is one of being nice to our neighbors, of giving to others, and of being a part of something bigger than we are.

Just so you know, I am writing this on a Wednesday night. All of my family is here, the house is full of sounds I haven't heard in awhile, and I am happy. Both of my children made it home, and boy number one brought future daughter-in-law number one with him.

I miss my kids a lot. So much that I recently got a puppy. They both bring me joy, but Otis, my new puppy, couldn't quite figure out on this day why he wasn't the center of attention. There will come a day soon when getting them all together will be impossible.

To me, Christmas is about recognizing the importance of family, even if for some reason you are separated from yours. This will be the first Christmas we will celebrate since my mother died. I know in some way, that will make the holidays different, but I am satisfied that she is watching from heaven and has every intention of helping us all know that it is okay to carry on without her.

Life changes. This year will be different than last, and next year promises to be the same. To me, Christmas is about recognizing that there are a lot of differences in this world. But, the common bond of humanity makes us more the same than different.

There is a lot of suffering this year with more people out of work than we have experienced in awhile. Good people can't make their house payments. Food pantries are under-stocked because more of our friends and neighbors are utilizing them. Good jobs are hard to come by. Some folks I know are working for free just to have something to do.

To me, Christmas is about recognizing how much those of us have who are blessed to be working steady jobs with steady paychecks. We all have bills to pay, but for those of us who have more than we deserve, Christmas is a time to share our good fortune with others. Be it a red kettle outside a retail store, a little extra in the offering plate on Sunday, a helping hand to someone who is down on his luck, or just a smile and a kind word to a stranger, Christmas is about recognizing the significance of giving to others.

I was recently diagnosed with prostate cancer. I went to the doctor last week, and the last test I underwent brought nothing but good news. The cancer is completely contained within the prostate, and the doctor is convinced that I am going to be cured.

I am too.

I also know that a lot of people have been praying for me. People I don't even know. People who are close friends. I am convinced now more than ever that prayer is powerful, and it works.

To me, Christmas is a celebration of the birth of The Christ Child, the King of Kings - a Savior for the world who requires nothing more of us but to acknowledge his authority over our lives and accept Him as a personal savior. I am a sinner. I wish it were not true, but it is. And in spite of my faults, Jesus loves me enough to put people in my life who will intercede with Him on my behalf that I might be cured of one of life's most dreaded diseases.

I don't know what God has planned for my life, but I do know that He has granted me another Christmas to contemplate how I want to serve Him in the coming year. To me, Christmas is about seizing the opportunity to make a difference.

Sometimes I think about why I get out of bed in the morning. I promise you it is not so that I can go to work and provide for my family. Perhaps it should be, but I believe I get out of bed every morning because I think I can help people through the gifts and talents I have been given. I really think I can make a difference.

Maybe it will be through my work in the church. Possibly it will be through my service with the local Chamber of Commerce. Even still, it may be through some chance happening with a stranger on the street. It is altogether possible that I may change the world because of the work I do.

But one thing is certain. I still believe I can change the world!

Whatever Christmas is to you, it is my hope that your Christmas season will be filled with peace, love, and joy. Perhaps under those conditions, we can change the world together.

The Sights and Sounds of a Rowland Christmas

I AM SITTING AT MY DESK as I write this column, and the signs of Christmas are all around me. The tree is sparkling in the corner with more packages underneath it than there is room. Perfectly wrapped boxes line the entertainment center that serves as overflow parking for the evidence that life is good at the Rowland House.

Voices and laughter waft up to my workspace from the living room below as the sounds of happiness and contentment fill our small living space. Otis and Charlie, my dog and his Tallahassee counterpart, stand with their noses pressed against the front door looking in from outside.

In case you didn't know, Charlie belongs to my son and daughter-in-law. At the door, the dogs have their heads cocked to one side as if to communicate their wonderment over all of the activity going on beyond the glass.

Rain is lightly falling, the temperature is more like early spring or late fall, and Santa's sleigh may need four- wheel drive this year instead of snow rails. The sound of wrapping paper crinkling around more boxes is only trumped by the clinking of pots and pans to signal that Mama is busy in the kitchen providing for her brood.

Everyone in the room has the same last name except one, and that is soon to change. My Navy son made it home from Chicago, brought with him an engagement ring, popped the question immediately followed by the popping corks of a couple of Champaign bottles.

My chemist son and his wife made it home for the big "pop the question" event, and I suspect we may be some of the few parents who manage to turn a son's engagement moment into a spectator sport. Both of our boys thought enough of us to include us in their moment, and at this point in my life, that means more than any present under the tree.

By the way, I didn't hear what she said, but she took the ring. I think that is code for "yes!"

Bing Crosby is softly singing Christmas Carols in the background, and the chatter in the room is all about what it means to be happy and thankful for the station in life to which we are assigned.

I can't help but think about the fact that the sights and sounds of that night so long ago for which we celebrate this season were so much different than those around my house this day. Barn animals and hay framed the most probable uncertainty and fear that faced Mary and Joseph as they prepared to bring a Savior into the world.

There is much debate, I guess, about what the Christmas season is all about, if there really is a Santa Clause, and if reindeer really fly. Do elves build the toys, or is it just Capitalists out to make a buck in a world that sometimes values stuff more than relationships or commitment?

Who has the best rendition of White Christmas? Bing Crosby or the Statler Brothers? What is eggnog anyway, and is it really necessary? Christmas cookies or candy canes? That one is a toss-up.

Should we say Merry Christmas or Happy Holidays; is it a Christmas Tree, a Holiday Tree, or just a sappy old pine tree?

Did the Grinch really steal Christmas or did Christmas change the Grinch? Who has the greatest rendition of the Christmas story? Luke or Linus?

But, here's the thing...and there is really no getting around it. The Christmas season is about the birth of a Savior, given of God, who lived a life on Earth, died for our sins, and was resurrected so that we might live beyond this world.

It sounds kind of trite when you say it, but Jesus really is the reason for the season. And as I take inventory of all of the good gifts to be opened this day, the   gift of knowing that God has blessed me and my family with all of those sights and sounds I mentioned earlier is the best gift of all.

Mike Rowland

All of us at the Rowland house would like to take this opportunity to wish each of you a very Merry Christmas and a blessed holiday season. It is our sincere hope that you will find peace, happiness, and comfort in the joy of the birth of a Savior who is Christ the Lord.

Acknowledgements

THE PROBLEM WITH THANKING PEOPLE IS that someone always gets left out. I owe a tremendous debt of gratitude to the late Dr. Ray Bruce. Ray and Edith Grimsley taught the first course at UGA I took in my Educational Leadership program. They were instructional leaders of the highest order, and it was Ray who first told me I could write.

Keith Barlow and Natalie Davis at the Milledgeville Union Recorder gave me a shot at the weekly column thing. I have always figured newsprint to be too precious a commodity to waste on the likes of me. They keep accepting my work, however, so I just keep sending it. I suppose they will let me know when my time is done. Until then, I am grateful for their loyalty and commitment.

My family has borne the brunt of most of the stories I have told over the years. Their willingness to be the public focus of my passion is hard to understand but much appreciated. I honestly couldn't have done it without you. Steven and Brian let me write them letters at key milestones in their lives. It is one thing to get a private message in your gym bag that you discover after returning to college or after ball practice. It is quite another to have it published in a newspaper that at least has a readership of mostly people you don't know. You guys are, and will always be, the loves of my life.

Meghan and Morgan signed up to take care of my guys. They didn't know becoming the object of the written word was part of the gig. Thanks for being great sports and tolerating an old man's passion for communicating. The one thing we will always have in common is the love for my sons.

My mother was always my greatest fan. She died in 2009 after a long battle with lung cancer. For a long time, I thought her contributing role in my life was to teach me the way not to do things. Her bull in a China shop style kept things stirred up most of the time. At this stage of my life, I am learning we are more alike than different. I miss her a lot, and I wish she could be here to see this.

My sister, Marsha, took her place, and I appreciate all of the publicity she has generated by forwarding my columns on to friends and co-workers via e-mail. For two people that fought like cats and dogs growing up, we have become steadfast friends in our waning years. I wouldn't trade that for all of the New York Times Best Sellers in the world.

If I have any degree of reason in my approach to life, it was given to me by my father. He generally seemed to be the voice of reason when a rebellious teenager took on his mother over just the kinds of things that teenage boys fight over with their mothers. He encouraged me to chase my dreams in ways that he may never know. As of this writing, he is 80 years old, still looking after himself, and a joy to be around. I will never be able to thank him enough for the many years of encouragement.

I need to thank my good friend and Great American Pat Schofill. Without his willingness to do things on a whim, some of these stories would have never occurred. Also, many thanks to Toby Hill, my sometimes boss, often times mentor, and always friend. His wisdom is infused throughout these pages.

Most authors thank their editor, publisher, or proof reader. They talk about manuscripts and the countless people who reviewed and contributed to their work. Around here, we are pretty much a one woman show. My wife, Trudy, has served as my proofreader, editor, publisher, and cheerleader for more than 30 years. She fixes my spelling mistakes, corrects my grammar, all of which I prefer to think of as typos. She is quick to tell me when I haven't done my best work, but when she is happy with my writing, well, it is usually a homerun. This book is a direct result of her year-long commitment to see it through. They say behind every successful man is a great woman. In my case, no words are truer. A good friend taught me that love isn't defined by what we go through; it is how we come out on the other side that matters most. We have been through a lot, and I like the view looking back from the other side.

Finally, if you have been the inspiration for something in this book, then please accept my sincere gratitude for your contribution. Who knows? You may get a part in the made for TV version.

Peace to all.